Emma Carroll

LETTERS FROM THE LIGHTHOUSE

ff
FABER & FABER

First published in 2017
by Faber & Faber Limited
Bloomsbury House,
74–77 Great Russell Street,
London WC1B 3DA

Typeset by MRules
Printed by CPI Group (UK) Ltd, Croydon CR0 4YY

A CIP record for this book
is available from the British Library

ISBN 978-0-571-32758-4

FSC
www.fsc.org
MIX
Paper from
responsible sources
FSC® C101712

'Engaging and entertaining.'
Independent on Sunday

'An **adventure** of old-fashioned charm.'
Sunday Times

'Perfect for **captivating** the imagination.'
Mumsnet

'**Absorbing**... brimming with atmospheric detail.'
Carousel

'My go-to author for historical fiction.'
The Bookbag

'Rich in **thrilling** details.'
Lovereading4kids

'Compelling.'
Metro

'Absorbing, sensitive and **genuinely magical** in feel.'
Independent

'A fast, exciting read.'
The School Librarian

'If your middle grade kids (ages 8-12) haven't discovered
Emma Carroll yet, then they're **missing out**.'
Irish Times

'Beautiful.'
Luna's Little Library

By the Same Author

Frost Hollow Hall
The Girl Who Walked on Air
In Darkling Wood
The Snow Sister
Strange Star

About the Author

Emma Carroll was a secondary school English teacher before leaving to write full time. She has also worked as a news reporter, an avocado picker and the person who punches holes into Filofax paper. She graduated with distinction from Bath Spa University's MA in Writing For Young People. *Letters from the Lighthouse* is Emma's sixth novel. She lives in the Somerset hills with her husband and three terriers.

To Claire B and Emma S,
who helped me with a story that wasn't mine to tell

KEEP CALM AND CARRY ON

We were halfway through the news when the air raid started. It was a Friday in January: we were at the Picture Palace for the 6 p.m. showing of *The Mark of Zorro*. All month the Luftwaffe had been attacking us, their bombs falling on London like pennies from a jar, so the fact they couldn't hold off for just a few measly hours made me hate the Germans that little bit more.

The cinema trip had been my sister Sukie's idea, as most things were. We were all in need of cheering up that evening: after the tea we'd just eaten at home it was a wonder we were still alive.

'It's like brains,' Cliff, my eight-year-old brother, said, lifting the pan lid to show us. It was probably only minced meat and potatoes, but you never knew with Mum's dinners, especially the ones you had to reheat when she was working late. And Cliff relished gory details, being the sort who'd pick scabs off his knee just to see what was underneath.

'Well, you *never* get scabby knees, Olive,' he once said to me, like it was the biggest character flaw in the world. The truth was I preferred reading books to running about in the street. I didn't see it as a weakness, either.

But we had to eat the horrid supper, of course. No one chucked food away with a war on, not even stuff that resembled brains. You simply pinched your nose and swallowed hard, then glugged down a glass of water. Afterwards, Sukie, being the eldest and in charge, said we deserved a trip out. She'd already seen the film last week with a friend.

'It's the cat's pyjamas. You'll both love it!' she gushed, as we went around the house closing the blackout curtains. Then to me, teasingly: 'Cheer up. It's going to be fun!'

People were always telling me I had a serious face, because I was dark and thoughtful-looking like my dad. What they really meant was I wasn't as pretty as Sukie, and I didn't mind because I was proud of my big sister, not jealous. She was just as marvellous on the inside – everyone seemed to think so.

'Is that better?' I beamed up at Sukie so she could tell how thrilled I was to be going out, especially with her. We didn't see nearly enough of her any more. She'd recently got a penpal and acted mysterious when letters postmarked 'Devon' arrived addressed to her. We'd all guessed who she was writing to: our next-door neighbour Gloria had a younger sister called Queenie, who was nineteen and lived in Devon. Having a penpal was, according to Sukie, all the rage.

And like she was with anything new, Sukie threw herself into it, kicking off her office shoes each night after work, then disappearing to her room to write. It wasn't the same as when we'd sent letters to Dad, where we each got to add our own line on the official blue army paper. Sukie shut her door on us. These were her letters – hers and Queenie's. I often wondered what they had to say to each other that was so private, and took up so much time.

Once we'd got our coats and grabbed our gas masks from where they hung in the hallway, we were ready for the cinema. It was a cold, damp evening and we were all done up in woolly hats and scarves. Cliff's mittens, on string threaded through his coat, dangled limp at the end of his sleeves, and he flapped them like wings to make me laugh.

Such was my excitement, I didn't think to ask why Sukie was buttoning up Mum's best green checked coat rather than her own. She'd done her hair different too, curled like a film star's, and was wearing postbox-red lipstick. It made her look older than seventeen and rather like Mum – the Mum before Dad died, who'd styled her hair and worn make-up and could argue for England.

*

By the time we reached the Picture Palace, the lights were already dimming. We'd only just found our seats – Row K, plush velvet that prickled the backs of your knees – when the great maroon curtains swung apart with a squeak.

First up was the newsreel. Every film show started like this, with five minutes of news from home and abroad. It was all very upbeat, with a proper English voice telling us everything would be all right, even if the film footage showed bombsites and battlefields. I watched eagerly, chin in hand, as the big white titles and the word 'Pathé' filled the screen.

Sukie, though, leaped to her feet.

'Stay here,' she whispered to us. 'If I'm not back in two minutes, meet me in the foyer when the film's over.'

Just like that she disappeared.

'She needs the lav,' Cliff said knowingly. 'That supper's giving her grief.'

'You're disgusting, you are,' I replied, not taking my

eyes from the newsreel. The footage was of men in RAF uniforms walking across an airfield. Immediately, it made me think of Dad.

In August last year we'd had a telegram from the War Office, telling us Dad's plane had been shot down over France. Six long months had passed, of every day hearing someone in my family crying, and Mum getting sadder and thinner. I couldn't sleep through a whole night any more. Often I barely slept at all.

'Look for the light,' Dad used to say when things were difficult.

I did try. He'd died for his country, people said. He was a hero. Watching the news helped me believe this was true, and as I listened to what a mightily fine job 'our boys' were doing, I could feel myself filling up with pride.

Tonight's news switched from RAF men to a city somewhere abroad – I didn't catch where. The footage showed hungry-looking people queuing for food, flanked either side by soldiers. There was snow on the ground. The people in line wore star-shaped badges on their coats.

Watching, I began to feel uncomfortable instead of proud. The Pathé news voice – jolly and brisk – jarred with what I was seeing. These people weren't just hungry but *scared*. I could tell by their faces how desperate they were, and it made me horribly guilty for the fuss we'd made about our supper.

Abruptly, the film stopped. The lights came up.

I blinked at the announcement on the screen:

AIR RAID IN PROGRESS.
PLEASE LEAVE THE THEATRE IMMEDIATELY.
HEAD TO THE NEAREST SHELTER.

'Blast it,' I said, reaching for my coat and gas mask. 'Come on, Cliff, we'd better find Sukie.'

People began to leave, though not very quickly. All around us seats thudded as they flipped upright. Coats were shaken out, hats pinned in place. There was a fair bit of complaining going on too.

'Should we ask for our money back?' asked Cliff.

'What?' I was still half thinking of those poor people in the newsreel. 'Oh, we'll ask Sukie. Keep hold of my hand.'

Weaving through the crowds we headed for the foyer. It was then the seriousness of our situation sank in. Beginning to worry, I told myself this was no different from any other raid – and they were happening almost every day now. Most of the action was down near the docks; on Fairfoot Road where we lived, they'd been more of an annoyance, forcing you out of bed in the middle of the night and into a freezing-cold air-raid shelter.

In the foyer, the lights were off. All I could see were the outlines of the front doors and the cash desk just inside. Already the space was filling up with people – but our sister wasn't one of them.

'She can't still be in the lavs.' Cliff's hand felt sticky in mine.

'She's probably powdering her nose,' I said, with a confidence I wasn't feeling. 'You've seen how glammed up she is tonight.'

'She's the dead spit of Mum.'

'She's got her best coat on, that's why.' I tapped my foot anxiously. 'Oh come on, Sukie.'

As the last few people came out into the foyer, the mood seemed to change. People were hurrying, jostling into those already making their way out.

'Stop pushing!' a man shouted like he was in charge. 'We'll get you all out, just slow down!'

Holding Cliff's hand even tighter, I wasn't sure what to do: stay and wait for Sukie, or go with everyone else to the nearest shelter. Someone was shining a torch at the floor to help guide people's feet. Then that went out too. A woman screamed, and though no one else joined in, you could feel the panic building.

I took a deep breath, trying to keep calm. 'Stay here, Cliff. I'm going to find—'

A hand came down heavily on my shoulder. 'You, lassie, and you, laddie.' It was the man in charge. 'What you dithering here for?'

I tried to explain: 'My sister's in the toilet.'

'I've just checked the lavs. Ain't nobody left inside but us, sweetheart.' The second voice was a woman's.

Two sets of hands steered us towards the door. Before I could shrug them off, we were out on the pavement. The noises, the smells of burning hit me at once. I felt a jolt of pure, cold fear. Up in the sky, searchlight beams criss-crossed the darkness. Already, I could hear the faint *crack-crack* of our guns as the German aircraft got closer, and fought the urge to cover my head protectively with my arms.

'I don't like it, Olive,' Cliff muttered.

I didn't, either. And until we found Sukie I was the big sister, the responsible one. That was pretty alarming too.

'Don't worry,' I told him, a stupid thing to say but it was all I could think of. 'Sukie's probably waiting for us in the shelter.'

We hurried down the street after the last few

stragglers. By now the roads were almost deserted. On the corner, an air-raid warden waved frantically, the white stripes of his uniform dimly visible in the blackout.

'Hurry up, you lot!' he shouted. 'What you waiting for, Christmas?'

Still holding Cliff's hand, I crossed the road. Thankfully there in front of us was the tube station, busy with men, women, a few little children, who were heading through the entrance with packets of sandwiches and pillows under their arms. Moving amongst the crowd was a Women's Royal Voluntary Service person in her navy blue uniform, hurrying people inside.

'Come on, you two,' she said, seeing Cliff and me on our own without a grown-up. I was glad to have an adult take charge. 'There's going to be cake and board games laid on tonight. It'll be quite a party down there!'

Cliff, liking the sound of it, reached out to take her hand; in doing so he let go of mine. He was only a few paces ahead of me, going down the steps with the nice WRVS lady. I just happened to glance behind. At a sound. At a sense. *Something.*

There was Sukie, looking around in panic. The relief made my legs go weak.

'Sukie!' I yelled, waving madly. 'Over here!'

She was running away from the shelter. And fast too – faster than I'd ever seen her run before – her arms pumping like pistons. She didn't turn, or slow down. I don't think she even heard me.

The air-raid warden was yelling now. 'Bomb incoming! Get down!'

He threw himself on to the pavement. I wasn't quick enough. The telltale whistling came next ... An eerie silence ...

Then a *WHUMP* as the bomb hit just a few hundred yards away. The ground rocked underneath me. Air was sucked from my chest, making me gasp and stagger backwards, though somehow I stayed on my feet. Glass smashed, bricks fell, planes droned onwards. Everything swirled dizzily together. For a moment I didn't know which way the sky was.

As the dust cleared, my stunned brain did too. Twenty yards or so up ahead was my sister. She was limping slightly, with one of her shoes missing, but still rapidly disappearing down the street.

'Sukie!' I cried again in frustration. 'Wait! We're here!'

She was searching for us, I was certain, and knowing her, she wouldn't think to keep herself safe. She'd stay out here, not giving up until she found us. This was what terrified me. Cliff would be all right in the shelter with the WRVS lady. What mattered was getting hold of Sukie.

Side-stepping the air-raid warden as he got unsteadily to his feet, I ran after my sister. The warden shouted something, I didn't hear what.

'Sukie! Slow down!' I cried, gas-mask box bouncing at my hip.

She was too far ahead. A silly, random thought came to me of how nice her hair still looked as it swung against the green of Mum's coat. Then panic. I'd never catch up with her. I'd a stitch in my side and even hobbling with one shoe, she was still too quick for me.

This part of the road had already been badly hit. The air was thick with brick dust and smoke, making me cough horribly. The road, full of potholes, was lined either side with blackened, shadowy shop fronts. Smashed glass from blown-out windows scrunched beneath my feet, and there was water everywhere, gushing past my feet. My ears were ringing. I felt light-headed too, as if everything was unreal – like I was watching myself in a film.

Still the planes kept coming. *Whoosh*. Silence. You could count the beats between. Then *thud* as a bomb hit. I was angry at my own feeble legs for not going any faster, but eventually I had to stop. Doubling over, I gasped for breath. Up ahead, at last, Sukie was slowing down too. Thank goodness.

It was then I saw why.

Emerging from an alleyway was a man I didn't recognise. He was tall, with slicked-back hair, wearing a mackintosh belted tight around his middle. He looked wet through, like he'd waded through a river to get here. Sukie went right up to him and shook his hand. I stopped in the middle of the street, confused.

What was she *doing*?

They were talking now. It didn't look like a normal chat about the weather either, because their heads were close together and the man kept glancing behind him. He gave Sukie a piece of paper before taking her hand and squeezing it in both of his.

Was she out here searching for us, then? It didn't look that way.

All I knew was she'd left us in a hurry, and this was where she'd gone – not to the toilet or the tube station but to meet a young man. It was probably why she'd got glammed up in the first place. I didn't know whether to laugh or burst into tears.

'Sukie!' I yelled.

She spun round. A strange look flitted over her face. As the man shrank back into the shadows,

Sukie hobbled towards me, shaking her head.

'You shouldn't have followed me!' She sounded furious. Frightened. It made me scared too. I grabbed on to her coat sleeve; now I'd found her I wasn't letting go. As more planes droned overhead, she glanced worriedly at the sky: 'Oh hell! Get down!'

A terrific *WHUMP* pitched me forwards on my knees. All round I heard cracking sounds as windows bent inwards. Another bomb hit with a *THUMP*. Something heavy was falling nearby. I cowered down, too terrified to look.

A minute passed or it might've been an hour. I was too disorientated to be sure. When I did lift my head to look around the street was full of glass and water – a burst main soaked everything like a downpour. Sukie was nowhere to be seen. The ringing in my ears was deafening. Where the shop fronts had been before was now just a heap of smoking rubble.

I tried to stand. Only suddenly, there was nothing to stand *on*. The air filled with screaming and a horrid smell like burning hair. The sky flashed brilliant white. I felt myself lift up. Up and up like I'd never stop. There was no air to breathe. Then I was falling down again, very hard and very fast.

I don't remember the landing part.

MAKE DO AND MEND

'Aren't you the lucky one?' said an unfamiliar woman's voice.

My eyes didn't want to open. I'd been dreaming that Dad was here. He was standing at the end of the bed, resting his elbows on the bedframe, about to wish me 'Nighty night, old girl' like he always did. I was desperate for him to stay so I could hear those words, because I was sure then I'd be able to sleep right through the night again.

'Ssshh. You'll scare Dad away,' I said to the woman who was talking.

She was jolly insistent, though. 'Come on, dearie, wake up.'

She shook me, just once, and suddenly everything hurt, from my toes all the way to my back teeth. The disinfectant smell was unmistakable. Uneasily, I opened one eye, then the other, taking in the white curtains half pulled around my bed, the white sheets and the whiter-than-white apron-clad nurse who hovered at my side. It was all so bright it hurt to look at. She'd called me 'lucky', but I didn't see how.

'You're at St Leonard's Hospital,' the nurse said. 'The ambulance picked you up last night. Come all across town you have.'

Which meant it was Saturday. A whole day later. I felt a wave of panic.

'I'd better get home. My mum'll wonder where I am,' I said, trying to sit up in bed and failing miserably. 'Is my brother here? Is he all right?'

'Keep still or you'll pull your dressings off,' the nurse warned.

I began to cry.

She got cross with me, then. 'For pity's sake! You've only got concussion and cuts and bruises. There were plenty brought in last night who won't walk again.'

I'd an egg-sized bump on my forehead, so she told me, a whopping great bruise on my left hip where the explosion had knocked me off my feet, a few minor cuts on my hands. No wonder everything hurt. My stupid eyes kept on filling too.

'What about Cliff?' I needed to know he was safe. 'He was in the shelter, in the tube station. That wasn't hit, was it? He's called Cliff Bradshaw. He's only eight and—' I started sobbing again.

The nurse's face softened. 'The shelter wasn't hit. Don't worry, I'm sure your brother's fine, though why you weren't sensible enough to be in there with him, I don't know.'

Nor did I. In a big stomach punch of guilt it came back to me that I was meant to be looking after him.

'Don't you remember what happened?' the nurse asked.

'Bits of it,' I sniffed. 'But not much after we left the cinema.'

Mum was working late. I'd been at home with Sukie and Cliff, hadn't I? Eating something horrible for our tea, and we went to see a film which Sukie said we'd like, then the air-raid siren went off ... and then ... things started to get blurry.

As the nurse helped me sit up, I read the name badge pinned to her chest.

'Nurse Spencer,' I said, trying to stop crying. 'Does my mum know I'm here? Or my sister Sukie? If no one's home you could try next door.' Gloria, our neighbour, was good in a crisis, and right now I needed to see a friendly face.

'I'll try to find out, though we're rushed off our feet today. In the meantime, let's get you a nice cup of tea.'

*

Nurse Spencer came back without tea. One look at her and I knew she had bad news.

'Oh lord,' she said, closing the curtain behind her. 'Maybe you weren't so lucky after all.'

I wanted to pull the covers up and hide, then she might go away and take her awful news with her. But I couldn't bear not to know, either. 'It's not my brother? Or . . .' I gulped. 'My sister?'

'It's your mother. A bomb landed on the building where she was last night.'

The ringing sound was back in my ears; I wasn't sure I'd heard her properly. 'My *mother*?'

'Yes, it was a direct hit. You mustn't think that she suffered.'

She probably said this to every relative, every time, which I supposed was nice of her. The words, though, didn't sink in.

'The rescue crew found you in the street, holding on to a coat,' she explained. 'There was a name in the coat – Mrs Rachel Bradshaw. You told them it was your mother's, but there was no sign of . . .' She hesitated. '. . . Of anyone else with you.'

What coat? I couldn't remember a coat. Or how

I came to be holding it. In frustration, I began sobbing again.

Nurse Spencer patted my shoulder. 'Let me get you that tea, shall I? We might even have a spot of sugar to put in it.'

She left me staring at the curtains.

My mother was *dead*?

I'd last seen her yesterday leaving for work with Gloria. They both did shifts at a printing works in Whitechapel, and it being nice weather, they'd decided to walk rather than catch the bus. It was the first time since Tuesday Mum had got out of bed, and even then Sukie and her managed to argue.

'You should be resting,' Sukie protested. 'You're not giving yourself a chance to get well.'

'I rested for three days, didn't I? Stop fussing,' Mum snapped back.

Actually, what she'd mostly done was cry and stare at her bedroom ceiling which didn't seem very restful to me.

'You're working too hard, Mum,' Sukie kept on. 'The doctor said you should—'

'That doctor doesn't know what he's talking about.' Mum never did believe in doctors, and had only gone to see ours last week to stop Sukie nagging.

'Your mum needs to work, love,' Gloria said, trying to keep the peace. 'Don't fret. She'll be all right.'

'I'll be absolutely fine,' Mum agreed, though she didn't look it. She was pale as anything, and went out of the front door with her hat on the wrong way round. I couldn't believe this would be my last memory of her.

'Come on, drink this,' Nurse Spencer said, reappearing with a cup of tea.

As I sipped, she knelt beside my bed, pulling out a box from underneath that smelled smoky and was full of damp clothes. The pleated skirt and Fair Isle sweater were mine. There was a hair clip – also mine – and my lace-up brown shoes, and my navy coat that was too short on the arms. It was a massive relief to see something I recognised.

Then Nurse Spencer held up my mum's coat.

As the fog in my head started to clear, it was Sukie I was seeing: Sukie looking glamorous and grown-up as if she was making a special effort for someone ... Sukie leaving us at the Picture Palace ... Sukie disappearing off down a bombed-out street to meet a man I'd never seen before ... the burst water main making everything wet ... That was about all I could recall. The rest was still as dim as the cinema itself.

Further down the ward, a nurse had started shouting: 'It's not visiting hours! You can't just barge in!'

Someone was running, their footsteps getting closer. The curtain round my bed swished back. A thin woman in a blue skirt and sweater rushed at me.

'Olive! Oh, my darling! You're all right!'

The cup of tea went everywhere – up the curtain, on the bedclothes, all over Nurse Spencer's apron. A second nurse bustled into the fray.

'That's no way to carry on!' she cried. 'The poor kiddie's injured!'

Yet the woman with her arms round me didn't let go. She smelled so strongly of home, I thought I was dreaming again.

'Are you a ghost?' I said, staring up at her. 'Or just someone who looks like my mum?'

The woman was crying and laughing at the same time. 'You silly child!'

It was funny because she wrinkled her nose like Mum. And she had the same chipped front tooth.

'What on earth were you playing at, going out in an air raid?' She even sounded like Mum.

I glanced at Nurse Spencer, who raised her hands in disbelief. 'The notes that came in with your daughter, Mrs Bradshaw ... they must've made a mistake ...'

She shook her head at the other nurse, who backed silently away.

So the woman who looked like Mum *was* Mum.

It was all a bit much. My head began to throb and I shut my eyes.

'Olive,' Mum said, stroking my fringe. 'I need you to listen to me, and I need you to be brave.'

Opening my eyes again, I swallowed nervously. 'What's happened?'

'Your sister didn't arrive at work today.'

Sukie was a typist for an insurance company in Clerkenwell. She said it was the dullest job ever.

'Isn't today Saturday, though?' I asked.

'She was due in to do overtime. No one's seen her since she was with you and Cliff last night. She's missing.'

'Missing?' I didn't understand.

Mum nodded.

The nurse added rather unhelpfully: 'We've had casualties from all over London. It's been chaos. All you can do is keep hoping for the best.'

It was obvious what she meant. I glanced at Mum, who always took the opposite view in any argument. But she stayed silent. Her hands, though, were trembling.

'*Missing* isn't the same as *dead*,' I pointed out.

Mum grimaced. 'That's true, and I've spoken to the

War Office: Sukie's name isn't on their list of dead or injured but—'

'So she's alive, then. She must be. I saw her in the street talking to a man,' I said. 'When she realised I'd followed her she was really furious about it.'

Mum looked at me, at the nurse, at the bump on my head. 'Darling, you're concussed. Don't get over-excited now.'

'But you can't think she's dead,' I insisted. 'There's no proof, is there?'

'Sometimes it's difficult to identify someone after . . .' Mum faltered.

I knew what she couldn't say: sometimes if a body got blown apart there'd be nothing left to tie a name tag to. It was why we'd never buried Dad. Perhaps if there'd been a coffin and a headstone and a vicar saying nice things, it would've seemed more real.

This felt different, though. After a big air raid the telephones were often down, letters got delayed, roads blocked. It might be a day or two before we heard from Sukie, and worried though I was, I knew she could look after herself. I wondered if it was part of Mum being ill, this painting the world black when it was grey.

My head was hurting again so I lay back against the pillows. I was fed up with this stupid, horrid war.

Eighteen months ago when it started, everyone said it'd be over before Christmas, but they were wrong. It was still going on, tearing great holes in people's lives. We'd already lost Dad, and half the time these days it felt like Mum wasn't quite here. And now Sukie – who knew where she was?

I didn't realise I was crying again until Mum touched my cheek.

'It's not fair,' I said weakly.

'War isn't fair, I'm afraid,' Mum replied. 'You only have to walk through this hospital to see we're not the only ones suffering. Though that's just the tip of the iceberg, believe me. There's plenty worse going on in Europe.'

I remembered Sukie mentioning this too. She'd got really upset when she told me about the awful things happening to people Hitler didn't like. She was in the kitchen chopping onions at the time so I wasn't aware she was crying properly.

'What sort of awful things?' I'd asked her.

'Food shortages, people being driven from their homes.' Sukie took a deep breath, as if the list was really long. 'People being attacked for no reason or sent no one knows where – Jewish people in particular. They're made to wear yellow stars so everyone knows they're

Jews, and then barred from shops and schools and even parts of the towns where they live. It's heartbreaking to think we can't do anything about it.'

People threatened by soldiers. People queuing for food with stars on their coats. It was what I'd seen on last night's newsreel at the cinema. My murky brain could just about remember those dismal scenes, and it made me even more angry. How I hated this lousy war.

I didn't know what I could do about it, a thirteen-year-old girl with a bump on her head. Yet thinking there might be something made me feel a tiny bit better.

My mind drifted back to my sister and how I'd seen her with a strange man.

'Does Sukie have a boyfriend?' I asked.

'How should I know?' Mum answered irritably. 'She never tells me anything.'

MOTHERS: SEND THEM OUT OF LONDON

The following Wednesday I was allowed home from hospital. There'd still been no sign of Sukie, and it was strange coming back to our house and her not being here. In my darker moments I began to wonder if Mum was being realistic – perhaps my sister *was* dead. Maybe Mum knew and wasn't telling us. I watched her mood for changes, but the truth was she was always sad nowadays so it was hard to tell.

At a loss as to what else to do, I decided to investigate the boyfriend possibility. Sukie had obviously planned to meet someone that night, someone who she'd dressed up for, who'd given her a note. Perhaps it'd been a love letter!

Excited by my theory, I asked Cliff what he thought.

'Ugh! A *boyfriend*? *Love letters?* That's disgusting,' he said, making sick noises.

So I didn't tell him what I found when, one afternoon as Mum slept, I tiptoed into Sukie's room and looked through her drawers. There were letters – loads of them tied up with ribbon and stuffed inside old chocolate boxes so they smelled of peppermint and toffee. All postmarked 'Devon', they were obviously from her penpal Queenie, though it wasn't these that caught my eye.

Underneath the chocolate boxes was a map. On seeing it, my heart gave a peculiar thud. There wasn't time to read it properly: hearing Mum stir in the next room, I knew I'd better get out of there quick. But not before I'd glimpsed a coastline and some foreign-sounding names.

I shut the drawer again feeling more confused, not less. Sukie hadn't mentioned going away, nor had she told us about a boyfriend. Perhaps she'd gone somewhere to be romantic with him, though I couldn't think where. It was winter still, for starters, and people didn't go on holiday these days, not with the war on. Yet it gave me hope thinking that's what she'd done, because holidays didn't last forever: people eventually had to come home.

*

Later that day Mum called Cliff and me to the kitchen. On the table stood two empty suitcases. Gloria from next door was sitting in a chair, drinking tea. Seeing my forehead she gave a low whistle. 'Jeepers, Olive, that bruise is all the colours of the rainbow.'

'She's got concussion,' Cliff said proudly.

'*Had* concussion,' I corrected him.

Gloria winked at me: 'Don't you let Jerry get away with it, my girl. Make sure you give him what for.'

'Jerry' was what Dad and his army pals used to call Germans, and little reminders like this often made me sad. But it was hard to feel glum with Gloria in our kitchen. She was one of those big, bright people you couldn't help but like, whose throaty laugh made you smile. She was Mum's best friend, and she'd become a sort of auntie to us, not having kids of her own or a husband – 'he ran off with the circus,' she told me once. I didn't know if it was true.

As Mum moved about the kitchen making tea, I sat down next to Gloria.

'Do you know anything about Sukie having a boyfriend?' I asked her.

She gave me a funny look – alarmed, almost – before glancing over her shoulder at Mum.

'Best not to mention your sister at the moment,' she

whispered, leaning towards me. 'Your mum's feeling fragile about the whole business.'

I sat back in my seat. It was then I properly took notice of the suitcases on the table. Cliff was *click-clicking* the catches and asking Mum if we were going somewhere nice.

'Hopefully.' Mum twisted her wedding ring, which meant she was nervous. 'After what happened to you, Olive, and ... to Sukie ... I've had to accept it's really not safe for you to stay on in London.'

Now I was nervous too, because I'd guessed what the suitcases were for.

'You're *evacuating* us, aren't you?' I said in surprise. 'But you can't. I mean ... you need us here ... *we* need to be here.'

That was always what Mum said. We *needed* to be together, especially after Dad went off to fight. When war was declared, all the schools round our way closed. Our classmates and our teacher Miss Higgins got evacuated to Kent and for a while I'd get postcards from my friends Maggie and Susan, who told me all I was missing – which wasn't much by the sound of it.

'You know the raids have got worse these past few months, darling.' Mum looked pained. 'It won't be for ever, I promise.'

I felt guilty when Cliff seemed so excited. He was already lifting one of the suitcases down from the table and bombarding Mum with questions.

'Will I have to share a bedroom? Will the people we stay with be nice? I hope they've got a dog – can we ask to be with a dog?'

'I don't know,' Mum kept saying. 'You'll have to wait and see.'

Yet how could we leave not knowing where Sukie was? How could I find out about her boyfriend from somewhere deep in the countryside? It was infuriating and disheartening and made my head ache.

'Lots of children get sent away,' Mum said, putting her arm round me. 'Some even have to move whole countries because of the war. You remember the Kindertransport, don't you?'

I did, vaguely. A year or so ago, at school, some children who couldn't speak English joined our class and we were amazed at how quickly they learned. They'd come over from Germany because, being Jewish, it wasn't safe for them there. Mum said they'd been blamed for all the bad things happening in their country, which was odd because lots of their parents were musicians and doctors and writers. You'd think their country would be proud of such clever people.

'So chin up, you won't be going too far – a train journey at most.' Mum kissed the top of my head, then looked distant again. 'The most important thing is that you're safe.'

'Are we going soon?' I asked.

'First thing Monday,' Mum replied.

I bit my lip: that was only a few days away.

'Where are we going, though?' Cliff wanted to know.

Gloria tapped the side of her nose. 'Leave that to me.'

Then her and Mum shared a *meaningful* look, the sort adults do when they don't want you to understand.

*

Cliff and me spent the weekend packing: underclothes, nightclothes, sweaters, socks, toothbrushes, combs. Though it still didn't seem right to be leaving, I couldn't deny the odd twinge of excitement. It'd been quite boring really, staying behind in London. The only people left on our street these days were babies, women and grumpy old men: there weren't even enough kids to play a game of hopscotch. I missed my classmates. There were even times when I'd missed going to school.

Who knew where we'd be this time next week?

Perhaps I'd make some new friends and Cliff might find himself a dog willing to sleep at the foot of his bed.

Mum told me to limit the books I took.

'Just take three,' she said. 'You won't be able to carry your case otherwise.'

But wanting all my favourites with me, I couldn't choose, so I packed five when she wasn't looking. I also took the seashell Dad had once given me, that sat on my window and had the sound of waves in it when you put it to your ear.

Once packed, we checked our things off from the list our local billeting officer had given out and which'd been unread in the kitchen drawer since the war began. The official government information said we had to wear school uniform for our journey. After a year at the back of our wardrobe, Cliff's short trousers hung high above his knees, and my pinafore would barely do up. There was also the question of my winter coat, which looked decidedly shabby.

'I can't send you off looking like that,' Mum said, eyeing me critically. 'You'd better have my smart one. It's decent and warm, and it's silly not to make use of it.'

Even so, I almost didn't take it. The smell on the collar was Sukie's smell, and it made a lump come to my throat. Yet when I put the coat on and turned back the cuffs a bit, I could almost imagine how she'd felt that night wearing it: strong and brave. By the time I went to bed on Sunday night, I was almost looking forward to the morning.

THE ROUND-UP

Early Monday morning we caught the bus to Paddington Station. As was usual these days, I'd barely slept a wink. For once, though, there was a bit of good cheer in the air, and with the fish paste sandwiches Mum had made us for the journey it felt almost like we were going on a day trip. Gloria, who'd come along to keep our spirits up, also had news to share.

'I've done a bit of asking about,' she said, 'and managed to sort a very nice place down in Devon for you both to stay. It's by the sea and—'

'Are we going to stay with your sister?' I blurted out.

Mum rolled her eyes. 'Let her finish, Olive.'

'It's all right.' Gloria smiled. 'Yes, you're going to Queenie's.'

I grinned, delighted. This was *good* news because, being Sukie's penpal, Queenie might know something about her disappearance, or be able to shed light on my boyfriend theory. She might even be able to explain about the map. Besides, going to stay with someone who knew my sister meant we'd not be living with a total stranger. I'd never met Queenie, but I knew she'd taken on running the village post office after her and Gloria's parents died. She was only nineteen, so it was a big responsibility, but Gloria said that's what the war did to people – it made them grow up fast.

'What d'you think, Cliff?' I gave him an enthusiastic nudge. 'We're going to stay by the sea!'

He looked up from the *Beano* comic he was reading. 'Can you see the beach from the house?'

'Better than that, Cliff: you can see the lighthouse,' Gloria replied.

Cliff and me shared an excited look: a lighthouse!

'Queenie's place is enormous – attics, cellars, the works,' Gloria went on. 'And it'll be nice to travel down with the other children being evacuated, won't it, eh?'

'*Other children?*' This threw me rather. 'I thought they'd all gone already.'

'From your school, yes. A few schools stayed open in other parts of the city, but it's got so bad lately they've been told to leave as soon as they can.'

*

The noise hit us the moment we left the bus. Coming from inside the station, it sounded like a school assembly only twenty times louder. Even the loudspeaker making crackly announcements couldn't deaden the racket of hundreds of high-pitched voices all talking at once.

'Gosh.' I gulped. 'That sounds like *a lot* of children.'

'It'll be fun for you, not being the only ones on the train,' said Mum, straightening Cliff's collar.

I wasn't so sure: more likely it'd end up being an almighty crush, and I worried about losing Cliff in the crowds. This time I'd make certain we didn't let go of each other.

Inside the station under the huge glass roof canopy, things got more overwhelming. A sea of different school hats – straw boaters, blue bowlers, woolly green berets – stretched as far as you could see. Being the only ones here from our school, we didn't have a teacher, so we stood near a group that did, hoping the billeting officer who was handing out labels would tell us what to do.

'I don't understand where I'm to tie it,' said a girl in brown uniform.

Her teacher looked ancient – at least forty – and was crotchety in that way old people can be. 'Oh for heaven's sake, Esther Jenkins, *do* listen to the instructions.'

The second his back was turned, the girl and her friends swapped labels, so Esther became Dorothy, and Dorothy – whoever she was – became Mabel, until the whole group was giggling. It was quite funny really, except I was too on edge to laugh.

Eventually the billeting officer in her green army jacket and skirt reached us.

'Names, please,' she said, checking her extremely long list.

'Olive and Cliff Bradshaw, staying with Queenie Pickering,' Mum replied.

'Budmouth Point. That'll be coach D,' the woman said, then to us: 'Make sure you sit in the right coach, please. Mr Barrowman's going with you. When you get there he'll be teaching you in the village school, isn't that nice?'

I nodded, already anxious that I'd forgotten something she'd said. Cliff was gazing about him with eyes on stalks, so I knew he hadn't even been listening.

'Look lively, Olive,' Mum said, jolting me from my thoughts. 'Put your name on the label.'

She'd dug a pencil out of her bag and I had to write my name, date of birth and home address. It was a brown card label with string attached, which I went to tie on my suitcase.

'No.' Mum stopped me. 'It's got to go on *you*.'

Right above our heads, a loudspeaker sprang into life: 'Platform twelve for the nine-fifteen a.m. service to Penzance. Platform twelve, the train is ready for boarding.'

I'd a feeling of wild terror that I wasn't ready. It was happening too fast. I wanted a bit longer to say our goodbyes, for it might be months or more before we saw Mum again.

'Now listen, darling,' she said to me. 'You're to look after your brother, all right?'

I wasn't sure I was capable of even looking after myself, but I nodded wretchedly. 'I'll try my best.'

'You'll be fine. You'll be together.' She forced a smile. It made me sadder to think we were leaving her on her own, but her job was here in London. She had to work to pay the bills, so we'd still have a nice home to come back to when these awful air raids were over.

The buzz of noise was becoming urgent. Children moved quickly now, teachers were shouting. I pressed a hand to my stomach, feeling it churn with last-minute nerves.

Mum and me both spoke at once: 'That's your train.' 'We'd better go.'

I hugged Gloria, who gave me a bag of toffees for the journey. I thanked her, then put my arms round Mum.

'Just a minute, let me check you both,' she said, pulling away. Taking out her hankie, she licked it, then wiped Cliff's cheeks, which he hated. Then she smoothed my fringe, even though it was already clipped aside. 'That's better. You're tidy, at least.'

I didn't want to look at her. But she took hold of my chin and gazed deep into my face. It was like she was trying to remember me, even though I was still there.

'Look after your brother, there's a good girl,' Mum said again, sounding like she had a cold coming. 'Write to me, won't you?'

I nodded. 'Any news of Sukie—'

'Of course,' Mum replied hastily. 'But try to put it from your mind, darling.'

Gloria, I noticed, was biting her lip; it left lipstick smears on her teeth. Like they'd done at home in our kitchen, her and Mum shared one of those loaded grown-up looks. What it was all about, I didn't know. Nor was there time to ask. Our train was being called again, and Cliff was hanging impatiently off my arm.

'Go on, then,' Mum said, giving me a gentle push. 'Stick together. You'll be all right.'

I took a big breath, like I was standing on the edge of a wall trying to find the courage to jump.

'Come on,' I said to Cliff, taking his hand properly. As soon as we started moving, the crowds that surrounded us buffeted us towards the train. When I looked over my shoulder, Mum and Gloria had gone.

Most of the train doors were closed by now, though heads and arms still hung out of the windows. The guards, strolling up and down the platform, were telling everyone to take their seats.

Coach D was divided into three big compartments. Each one was full, smelling of heaters on too high and damp, dusty clothes.

Cliff looked like he might cry with disappointment. 'I wanted to sit by the window.'

I gave him a toffee and told him not to worry, though I didn't honestly think we'd get a seat at all.

Making our way down the train, we stepped over sprawled legs and enormous pairs of feet. They were older kids than us, in the uniforms of at least two or three different schools, who looked bored already and the journey hadn't even started. After searching the entire length of the carriage, we'd still not found a seat. So, putting our cases down flat, I told Cliff to perch on top of them. I'd be all right leaning against the wall – at least that was the plan. Sitting down, Cliff had just opened his *Beano* when a hand swooped in and grabbed it.

'Hey!' Cliff looked up.

'Give that back!' I cried.

At eye level was a label saying 'Dorothy Roberts', but the face above it belonged to that naughty girl, Esther Jenkins. Her hair was in two dark brown plaits, the pointed ends of which looked like they'd been sucked. She was holding Cliff's comic high above her head. It annoyed me that she'd taken it without asking.

'That's not yours!' I said, reaching for it.

'It is now.'

I tried to make a lunge for the comic, but she was taller than me.

'I bought that for the journey,' Cliff protested.

'Tough,' Esther said. She spoke a bit oddly, using English words but sounding foreign. 'It's ours now.'

Before we could do anything, the comic got passed on to a boy, then another boy, before disappearing down the carriage.

Esther patted Cliff on the head – 'Thanks, pal' – before going back to her seat. Cliff's bottom lip started to quiver.

'Sssh, don't cry,' I said, putting my arm round his

shoulders. 'We'll get it back.'

'Shut up, Olive! Leave me alone!' He turned away, burying his face in his arms. I didn't know what to do. There were no teachers on board to tell, though through the window I saw that same old one out on the platform, arguing with a guard. Sukie, I knew, wouldn't stand here feeling useless. Even worse, Cliff had started sobbing. I'd promised to look after him and was doing a lousy job of it.

'Stay there,' I told Cliff.

Heading down the carriage, I soon found the *Beano*. Two girls were poring over a Dennis the Menace cartoon on the centre pages.

'Umm ... excuse me,' I said politely, stopping at their seats.

The girls kept their heads down.

I tried again. 'I don't know if you realise but that belongs to us. You can borrow it if you want, when my brother's finished reading it.'

They ignored me. I felt rather stupid. Especially when the boys in the next row started laughing and jeering, egging people on to join in until it spread through the whole carriage.

Thoroughly flustered and wanting the whole thing to just be over, I tried to grab the comic again.

The carriage fell silent.

Standing in the doorway was a teacher, the one who'd been arguing on the platform. Now, it seemed, it was our turn.

'Carson! Mitchell! Don't you know your alphabet?' he barked.

The girls reading Cliff's *Beano* jumped out of their skins. As the comic slithered to the floor, I snatched it.

'You're supposed to be in coach F, not this one,' he yelled. 'I've just spent the last ten minutes trying to sort out the confusion you've caused.'

'But Mr Barrowman, sir ...' One of the girls tried to speak.

The teacher – *our* teacher, I realised dismally – cut her dead. 'Each coach is for a different location, you foolish girls. This is coach D, going to Devon. You're in coach F, which will be going to hell and back if you're not careful. So move yourselves. You're holding up the whole train.'

Mortified, the girls rose out of their seats and got their suitcases. The whole carriage watched without a word. I crept back up the aisle towards Cliff.

'You there! The girl in the checked coat!' Mr Barrowman barked.

I stopped. Turned round. 'Me?' Which was a stupid thing to say since no one else was wearing a checked coat.

'Take these.' He clicked his fingers at where the girls had been sat. 'Hurry up now.'

Cliff and me slid on to their still-warm seats. Reunited with his *Beano*, my brother soon cheered up. But right in my eyeline, just down the aisle, was the person who'd started it all.

'What you looking at?' Esther Jenkins mouthed.

'Dunno. Hasn't got a label on it,' I muttered to myself, though like all of us she had one swinging from her coat. I just hoped she'd lose interest in me once we got moving.

Walking up the aisle, Mr Barrowman checked our names against his own shorter list, and made Esther and Dorothy swap their labels. The moment he took his seat at the front, Esther Jenkins started on me again: 'You with the bruise on your forehead.'

I made a point of gazing out the window. She didn't take the hint.

'You snitched on my friends,' she said. 'They had to move carriages because of you. And now they won't be billeted with us, so I'd say that's your fault.'

It wasn't my fault, I knew it wasn't. I didn't make

them sit in the wrong part of the train. I didn't snitch on them either, yet Esther Jenkins blamed me and I felt hot and miserable with the injustice of it.

Settling back in my seat, I consoled myself with two thoughts: Queenie, at least, would be kind and friendly and might know more than I did about where my sister was. Plus I'd never seen a proper lighthouse before.

CARING FOR EVACUEES IS
A NATIONAL SERVICE

It was dark when we finally arrived, which wasn't a bad thing. I was tired of seeing cows. And fields. And trees. And little country stations hung with bunting and WRVS ladies rushing forwards to welcome the train, which had been exciting at first but after a while just made the journey seem longer. One by one, the carriages had emptied out and now, at last, it was our turn.

'Budmouth Point,' announced the guard. 'Train calling at Budmouth Point.'

Everyone was on their feet before the train had even stopped. In a scramble of suitcases, our entire carriage made for the doors. Mr Barrowman, shouting over our heads, told people to stop pushing.

'One at a time!' he hollered. 'Remember your manners. This isn't the Harrods sale!'

No one was listening. We were too eager to see what Budmouth Point was like, so in the end the guards simply opened the train doors and we tumbled out on to the platform.

There was no bunting, no WRVS women to greet us. It felt oddly quiet after the noise of the train, and for a moment, everyone seemed a bit stunned.

'You all right?' I asked Cliff, dumping his suitcase in front of him.

He nodded. 'Smells different here, doesn't it?'

He was right: the air smelled wet, salty. With a shiver of delight, I thought of the sea. Tomorrow we'd go to the beach, see the lighthouse, find seashells like the ones Dad used to bring us. In fact, I was beginning to feel quite hopeful, when two ladies in wellington boots appeared from the direction of the ticket office. They were having an argument.

'With all due respect, Mrs Henderson—'

'Are you telling me how to do my job, Miss Carter?'

'Of course not, but if she's a Kindertransport child…'

As Mr Barrowman cleared his throat, they broke apart with a startled 'Oh!'

'You must be our evacuees!' cried the shorter and rounder of the two women, as if we'd dropped from the sky. She looked like someone from a murder mystery story, the type who wore tweeds and drank sherry.

'Indeed, I suppose we must,' Mr Barrowman replied. He did sarcasm as well as any teacher.

'Then welcome to Budmouth Point!' She threw open her arms rather theatrically. A titter went through the group, which Mr Barrowman quickly shushed.

'I'm Mrs Henderson. I've lived here all my life. And this –' she indicated the other woman sniffily – 'is Miss Carter, who's been here *not quite a week.*'

Miss Carter was a lot younger than Mrs Henderson. She had blonde hair cut to her jaw, and looked thoroughly fed up. 'All I suggested was—'

Ignoring her, Mrs Henderson said, 'Allow us to escort you to the village hall where you'll be introduced to your host families.'

She made it sound just round the corner. In reality, it was a good half an hour's walk down a dark country road with only her and Miss Carter's torches to guide us. Away from the shelter of the station, I felt the full force of the wind, so strong you had to lean into it as you walked. One of the older boys started telling a ghost story called 'The Hairy Hands', and I could feel Cliff next to me, hanging on his every word. Worried he'd have bad dreams, I tried to walk faster so we'd be out of earshot. But up ahead was Esther Jenkins – a different type of nightmare – and I thought it best to keep out of her way.

By the time we reached the village, I'd blisters on my palms from my suitcase handle. Perhaps Mum had been right about those extra books, after all. I was ravenous too, and wondered what Queenie might've made for our supper. It was hard to see anything of Budmouth Point itself. The dark felt even thicker than the blackout in London, though I could just about make out the outline of houses on either side of the road.

'Crikey, it's so quiet here,' one of the girls observed.

'Budmouth Point? Budmouth *Dump*, more like,' Esther Jenkins muttered.

A few of the boys pretended to laugh. Cliff squeezed my hand, and I squeezed back just to let him know I was there.

Then I saw light. Not from Mrs Henderson's torch; this was something bigger, out beyond the houses. It wasn't constant like the searchlights over London, but every few moments sent out a beam so strong that in it I glimpsed the grey water and white-topped waves of what had to be the sea. My heart gave a little skip.

'That's the lighthouse,' said Miss Carter, who appeared beside me. 'Beautiful, isn't it? A beacon to guide the lost to safety.'

It *was* beautiful. I'd never seen a real working lighthouse before. The way its light reached far out into the darkness was mesmerising to watch.

Miss Carter sighed. 'There's talk of turning it off now, though. It's a threat to national security, apparently, because the enemy's been using landmarks like this to navigate their planes.'

'When they come over to bomb us, you mean?' I'd heard something similar back in London, about German pilots following the Thames to find their targets.

'Exactly that.'

This war, I thought bleakly. This horrid, horrid war. Even down here in the wilds of Devon we couldn't escape it.

*

Inside the village hall was a table laid for tea. It was a decent-looking spread – thick white bread with proper butter underneath the jam, and slices of dark crumbly fruit cake. But Mr Barrowman shooed us away from the table.

'We're not here to eat the locals out of house and home,' he said sternly.

'Can't we have some?' whispered Cliff, who I knew would be starving.

'No one else has, so we'd best not,' I answered. 'We don't want Queenie to think we've got worms.' At least people weren't lying when they said you got better food in the country. This lot looked wholesome and fresh, and gave me high hopes for what we'd eat tonight at Queenie's.

Behind the table stood a group of women, who I guessed were locals. Even the younger ones were still dressed in the long skirts and bell hats Londoners had worn in the other war, the one that ended twenty-two years ago.

'Which is Queenie?' Cliff asked.

I didn't know; I'd never seen a photo. In my head I pictured her as tall, like Gloria, with a warm, smiley face. Being Sukie's penpal, she was bound to be the fun-loving, lipstick-wearing, jitterbugging type, who'd be friendly and welcoming towards us.

It was bewildering that no one in the group fitted her description. *These* women didn't even smile. They were pointing at us evacuees – *discussing* us – like they were choosing what cake to have for tea.

'I'm looking for help with milking my Jerseys,' said a woman with large front teeth. 'Someone who's not shy of getting up at dawn.'

The older kids seemed to think this a right lark, especially the boys, most of whom had probably never been near a live cow before. Within moments, they were falling over themselves to volunteer.

'Don't take all the best ones, Poll,' another woman complained, which started them off bickering over who'd get the strongest boys.

It wasn't exactly fun, hovering like a spare part while everyone else got picked. There was no sign of anyone who might be Queenie, either. I grew anxious again, wondering how much longer we'd have to wait. Cliff leaned his head sleepily on my shoulder.

'D'you think she's forgotten us?' he yawned.

'Course not, you daftie.' I tried to stay cheerful for both our sakes. 'She's probably just adding the finishing touches to our supper.'

'What d'you reckon she's made us?'

I thought for a moment. 'Steak pie probably, with bread and butter pudding for afters.'

'And custard?'

I nodded. 'A whole jug full,' which made Cliff's stomach rumble so loud I actually heard it.

Yet as the hall began to empty and Queenie still didn't appear, I wondered if there'd been some sort of mix-up. Or perhaps she'd changed her mind about having us, being too upset about Sukie's disappearance, and we'd be put on the next London train home. I wished someone would tell us what was going on.

What unsettled me more was the sound of crying coming from the back of the hall, though I couldn't see who was making it: Mrs Henderson, Miss Carter and one of the local women blocked the view.

'You mustn't think like that,' Mrs Henderson was saying. 'None of this is your fault.'

'If anyone's to blame it's Hitler,' Miss Carter added.

'Every time I get settled, I have to move again.' The voice was a girl's, wobbly with tears. 'I liked it at the Jenkinses' house. It was . . . all right, you know?'

'Once the bombing stops you can go back to the Jenkinses again, can't you, eh?' said Mrs Henderson.

'But even that's not my real home, is it?' the girl sobbed.

'I know, lovey, I know,' soothed Mrs Henderson.

I still couldn't see the person crying, but with a start I recognised her voice. The strange, gruff twang was a giveaway, as was the name 'Jenkins'.

'Crikey,' I muttered under my breath. If someone as tough as Esther Jenkins could cry, there wasn't much hope for anyone else.

But for us and the little group surrounding Esther, the hall was now completely empty. I felt miserable. We might as well have stuffed ourselves with the bread and jam: no one would've noticed. I was about to take some for Cliff and myself, when Mrs Henderson looked round.

'Oh, you poor mites!' she gasped in surprise. 'You're still here!'

'Yes, we are,' I said dismally. I waited for her to say something, to tell us what to do, but she simply looked at her watch and frowned.

'So *is* Queenie coming for us?' I asked.

She let out a big bellow of a sigh. 'That's the plan, though goodness knows where she is. I can't wait here for ever; I've got my goats to milk.'

Cliff and me glanced at each other: why would anyone milk a goat?

'I specifically told her to be here at six,' Mrs Henderson continued. 'This isn't good. It isn't good at all.'

'Perhaps she got the day wrong,' I offered, though it sounded pretty feeble.

Mrs Henderson shook her head. 'It's those clocks of hers – very romantic but terribly impractical.'

I didn't know what Mrs Henderson meant, but I was

starting to realise my days of counting on grown-ups and big sisters were over. I was going to have to take charge myself.

I turned to Cliff. 'Buck up, let's grab our things, shall we? If Queenie won't come to us, we'll go to her.'

Which was all very well except we didn't know where the post office was.

Do Your Duty

The sight of us setting off into the dark brought Mrs Henderson running. Together, we soon found Queenie's house, which stood halfway down the main street. Just as Gloria predicted, you could see the lighthouse properly from here – or as properly as was possible in the dark.

'This is it,' Mrs Henderson shouted over the wind. 'The post office.'

Yet the post office part was only one small bay window with the blinds pulled down. The rest of the house towered above us, important-looking with wide steps leading up to a huge front door. My jaw dropped in amazement at the size of it.

'Blimey!' Cliff gasped. 'It's massive!'

Shivering with cold and tiredness and the last glimmers of excitement, I tucked my arm through his. 'Isn't it marvellous?' I couldn't wait to see inside.

Yet after three hearty raps on the front door Queenie still didn't appear.

'She'll be down in the cellar, unable to hear us,' Mrs Henderson muttered in annoyance. 'Knock on the glass, Olive, will you?' and she pointed to the left of the steps where, almost hidden by ivy and blackout curtains, was a cellar window.

I did as she asked. Finally, as we heard footsteps approaching from the other side of the door, a sudden bout of shyness came over me. The person I was about to meet was Sukie's penpal. She'd be wonderful, I was certain. I just hoped she didn't mind having us foisted on her, a pair of windswept, homesick kids.

The door inched open. From behind it peered a small, plain-looking woman who at first glance could've been fifteen or fifty. She was wearing an enormous green sweater that reached her knees. Assuming she was the housekeeper, I stared past her into the hallway.

'Your evacuees are here, Queenie,' Mrs Henderson said rather pointedly.

'My – ?' The woman clapped a hand over her mouth. 'Oh! Is it that time already?'

I put down my suitcase in surprise. So this was Queenie? I could see now she wasn't that old. She wore glasses and had freckles and reddish, poker-straight hair. I supposed I was expecting someone fashionable like Sukie, and she wasn't.

Clearing my throat, I stammered, 'We're ... ummm ... We live next door to Gloria in London. She ... umm ... arranged for us to come and stay.'

Queenie eyed us coolly. Her glasses were so thick it was like being stared at through a fish tank. 'You're rather weedy-looking. I was expecting someone stronger.'

I blinked, taken aback. Sukie always said I was *slender*, which sounded nicer even if it wasn't true.

Queenie brightened. 'Can you run? Who's the faster, you or your brother?'

'Umm ...' I stuttered. 'I'm not sure.'

'I was the fastest in my class at school,' Cliff chipped in.

'And even weedier than your sister, by the looks of you,' Queenie remarked.

Cliff stared at her, wide-eyed and open-mouthed. It was almost funny, except it was taking all my concentration now not to burst into tears.

Mrs Henderson sighed. 'For heaven's sake, Queenie, let the poor devils at least get inside. They're exhausted.'

'I'm checking their credentials,' Queenie replied sharply. 'I need workers, Mrs H. You know how busy it's been here since I lost the Jenson boys.'

'Who're the Jenson boys?' Cliff asked before I could.

Queenie ignored him. It was Mrs Henderson who explained: 'A couple of local lads who worked for Queenie in the shop, doing deliveries. They've been called up for the army.'

'I'll be expecting you two to pull your weight,' Queenie added. 'Call it the war effort if you like, but be warned: I've no time for idlers.'

My hopes of exploring the beach tomorrow faded, though I was willing to do my bit – *more* than willing – especially if it meant getting back at Mr Hitler. I'd lost my dad to this stupid war, which surely meant I had the right credentials. I'd have explained this too, had Mrs Henderson not given me a little shove in the direction of the door.

'In you go,' she said.

We stumbled inside. I was glad to be out of the wind at last. But as the door closed, I realised Mrs Henderson was no longer with us and I suddenly didn't feel so brave about being on our own.

'She's gone to milk her goats,' I reminded Cliff, who managed a feeble smile. Reaching for his hand, I put the last of Gloria's toffees in his palm.

Queenie took us into a hallway. There weren't coats or umbrellas or gas masks hung on hooks like at home. This hall smelled fusty as a church and echoed like one too, as the floor was paved with flagstones. The only light came from the candle Queenie held. It wasn't what I expected: none of this was.

'Follow me,' she said, leading us deeper into the house.

From the hall, we went up a staircase lugging our suitcases, satchels and gas-mask boxes. All day I'd built up an idea of Queenie in my head: the reality was ... *different* ... and, I had to admit, horribly disappointing. She hadn't remembered we were coming. She hadn't even mentioned Sukie, and she was supposed to be her friend. As for supper, I was beginning to give up hope.

At the top of the stairs, we trudged along a landing where the floor tilted and creaked, and where the dark grew ever darker.

'She's not on the electric, is she?' Cliff hissed in my ear.

'Doesn't look like it,' I agreed, wondering what else Gloria *hadn't* told us about her sister.

Finally, we stopped in front of another staircase, this one so steep it was almost vertical.

'I've put you in the attic,' Queenie said.

Beside me, I sensed Cliff stiffening up. He hated heights. And those stairs – slippery, painted, uncarpeted wood – looked capable of breaking necks.

'You'll want to unpack, I expect. Don't let me keep you,' muttered Queenie, though once she'd given me what was left of her candle it was obviously *us* keeping her.

Cliff and I shared a bewildered look.

'Um ... I don't mean to be rude,' I said. 'But are we having supper?'

'Are you expecting me to *cook*?' She made it sound like I'd asked for a trip to the moon.

'We haven't eaten since the train,' Cliff replied, swallowing his toffee in one gulp.

Queenie said nothing.

I knew when we were beaten. 'I'm done in, Cliff. Let's just go to bed.'

*

The attic stairs weren't as bad as all that. I made sure of it by insisting Cliff go first, so if he slipped I'd at least try to catch him. At the top were our bedrooms, two huge rooms that stretched the whole length of the house. There wasn't much furniture in mine – a bed, a chest of drawers, a bedside table, a rag rug on the floor. It reminded me of a horrid boarding school, the sort that naughty children get sent to in stories. Despite putting away my skirts and sweaters and arranging my hairbrush and clips on the bedside table, it still didn't feel homely. My books looked lost on the huge, wide windowsill. I didn't even unpack Dad's seashell.

Cliff's room was just as vast and cold, with a bed that sagged like a hammock. This I found out as I perched on it to wish him goodnight.

'It won't be for ever,' I promised. 'I'm sure we'll have a decent breakfast in the morning.'

Luckily, Cliff was already falling asleep. 'It's not that bad,' he mumbled into the pillow. 'Though I was really hoping she'd have a dog.'

It was Queenie's chilly welcome that sat uneasily with me. Odd that our sister – popular, fun, pretty as a pin-up – would be friends with someone who wore old droopy sweaters and didn't actually seem to *like* people very much. Other than being a similar sort of age, I couldn't think what they had in common.

Back in my room, I got into bed. The sheets, the pillowcases – everything felt damp with cold. Heaping all the blankets I could find over me, I climbed back under the covers and decided to write a postcard home to Mum; we'd all been given a pack of blank ones earlier by Mr Barrowman.

'Keep your messages cheerful,' he'd warned us. 'No homesick blubbing. No moaning about your hosts. Your parents have more important things to worry about than you lot.'

Blowing on my almost-numb fingers, I got to work.

Monday 10th February 1941

Dear Mum,

The train took seven whole hours, but it was jolly good fun meeting the other children on board.

Queenie's just how I imagined her – she's made us ever so welcome. We've got our own big bedrooms so Cliff's happy, though he wishes there was a dog here.

Lots of love, Olive x

Mrs Rachel Bradshaw

16 Fairfoot Road

Bow

London

England

The candle Queenie'd given me soon burned low. What helped was the lighthouse beam as it swept through the attic: count to six and it was dark, count another six and it went bright again, edging the blackout curtains with gold.

It didn't bring any heat, though, and once I'd done the postcard, I got out of bed and put on Mum's coat over my nightdress. It smelled faintly of Sukie still and something smoky and bitter. Giving it a big sniff, I breathed my sister in, though the smoke smell was stronger and I didn't like the way it reminded me of the air raid, filling my head with shadows.

Enough, I told myself. Go to sleep.

I couldn't get comfortable. The sandwich wrappers from earlier were still stuffed in my pocket, and every time I moved they crackled. In the end I took them out. Yet when I lay down again, the rustling noise was still there, coming from inside the coat. I checked the pockets again: both were empty.

What I could feel was something stuffed into the lining. Intrigued, I sat up, lighting the remaining stub of candle. I was now able to see loose threads in the seam below the pocket. A slit big enough to put my hand in … and pull out a folded-up piece of paper, though at first it looked so wrinkled I thought it was a tissue.

Then I saw the writing – it was big and clear and nothing like Sukie's own. It wasn't a letter. I wasn't actually sure *what* it was – and I spent a good few minutes staring at it. It looked like this:

```
DAY 9
I  26  8  T/U  I
J  26  9  16  19  12  6  8  I
B  26  T  -  50.26
B  12  13  20  +  3.6
```

I wondered if it was measurements, or a lock number, or a list of those plates that go on the front of cars. Yet the more I studied it, the more I felt uneasy, and certain.

It was some sort of code.

LEND A HAND ON THE LAND

'Breakfast is for time-wasters. We've got work to do,' Queenie announced the next morning.

She'd woken us so early it wasn't yet light, and we were standing in the post office, washed and dressed and bleary-eyed, wondering what the heck was going on. After a restless night considering Sukie's note, I decided to speak to Queenie as soon as I could. First, though, we simply *had* to eat.

'Don't worry, we can eat breakfast in two minutes flat,' I reassured her.

'Less than two minutes,' added Cliff.

But there was no sign of breakfast. Not even a cup of tea. Queenie, I decided, was in league with the enemy. No one British would starve children like this. As for time-wasting, I wasn't sure how she'd tell: the clock on the wall above the counter said ten past two, and was as dead as a doorknob.

Yet, despite my reservations about Queenie, the

shop itself looked normal. Rows of pigeonhole-type shelves to hold mail lined the walls. On the counter sat enormous weighing scales, and a box displaying hair combs for sale. It was the sort of place that sold anything and everything. The stock stood at the very front of the shelves, hiding the empty space behind. There were tins: shoe polish, peas, pilchards. Packets of soap flakes, dried beans, broken biscuits by the bag, and – I gulped hungrily – a glass-domed cake stand. On it were currant buns, yesterday's at least by the looks of them. As Cliff ambled over to inspect the buns, I seized my chance.

'I need to talk to you, Queenie,' I said, dropping my voice. 'About my sister. She's got a boyfriend and I think they might've been planning to run away and—'

'Good grief!' Queenie interrupted sharply. 'Don't tell me Gloria is sending *her* here too?'

'What?' I was confused. 'No, I didn't mean—'

'All right, one each,' she called to Cliff who, having lifted the dome off the cake stand, now had Queenie's full attention.

I wanted to ask her what she'd meant about Sukie – it was an odd remark to make about a friend. But the buns took over. True to our word they didn't last two minutes.

66

*

That morning I started my delivery job. In daylight, Budmouth Point looked prettier than I'd supposed – it wasn't a *dump* like Esther had said. There was a school, a church, a baker's shop, rows of little white cottages set into the hillside. Most of the larger houses were on the main street, which ran steeply down to a harbour. Beyond it, perched at the end of a long, cobbled wall, was the lighthouse.

I was to take groceries and post to those who, for whatever reason, couldn't collect it themselves. Cliff, being younger – and weedier – was to help serve customers in the shop. Queenie made him wear an apron that fell to his ankles, while I had to carry a leather delivery bag. She told us that though today was our first day she'd expect us to be as quick as the Jenson boys had been because customers shouldn't be kept waiting.

Before I went, she gave me two extra bits of advice. The first was: 'Ignore people if they stare. It's the Budmouth way. I've lived here all my life and they still gawp at me like I'm an intruder.'

I wondered if it had more to do with her sweaters.

'And,' she added, 'if you've ever reason to be on

the beach, don't go past the last groyne.' She meant one of those wooden fence things that ran out into the sea.

'Why not?' Cliff asked.

'Quicksands. They'll swallow you whole before you've a chance to even scream. It's a far worse death than drowning in the sea, so people say.'

Cliff's eyes went owl-wide. 'Wow!' As he turned to me, I guessed what he was about to ask.

'No, we're not going down there. Don't even think about it,' I told him very firmly.

*

Delivering was surprisingly hard work. By the end of the first day my calf muscles ached like mad, but it was a great way to get to know the layout of the village. At supper – bread and dripping, only one slice each – Queenie told me I was indeed as fast as the Jenson boys. Then she left us to clear away, so I didn't get the chance to ask about Sukie.

After we'd done the dishes, and were up in the attic by ourselves, I decided to show Cliff the coded note. We were sitting cross-legged on my bed. It was dark by then and the torch batteries were on the blink, but we could just about see the numbers and letters on the page. Cliff bent over the note eagerly, though it gave me a bad feeling, seeing it again, because I was sure it had something to do with Sukie's disappearance.

'Tatty, isn't it?' Cliff remarked.

'It got wet in the air raid,' I explained. 'What d'you think it says?'

'It's not another love letter, is it?' he said, holding it at arm's length.

'It's a funny sort of love letter if it is,' I remarked.

'Well, it's not telephone numbers?' he said. 'Or place names?'

I didn't think so. Really Cliff had no more of an idea than I did.

'It's probably just a silly joke she had with one of her friends,' I decided. Taking the note from him, I hid it at the very back of my sock drawer, though that didn't stop it troubling me.

*

'You've an extra delivery today,' Queenie told me on Friday, slipping a small package into the bag. 'Chicken for Mrs Drummond at 4 Salters Terrace. Tell her it's all I could get, though it might not be right.'

'That's at the very top of the village, isn't it?' I asked, just to check.

As the week had gone on, I'd got to know my way round the back lanes and cut-throughs. I had the sense Queenie was getting used to us too. Begrudgingly – and rather badly – she'd even started to cook for us. Yet apart from mealtimes, I didn't see that much of her. She'd either be in the shop or down in the cellar. When I tried asking about my sister, she'd stare at me blankly as if she'd forgotten who Sukie was. Other times, she'd cut across me with some delivery detail or job that needed doing.

That Friday morning was a case in point: 'Mrs Drummond'll need to return yesterday's bacon, all right? Dr Morrison's housekeeper says she'll have it on her meat ration, so if you could take it there, please.'

Not wanting to carry it all the way round, I left Mrs Drummond's delivery until almost last.

*

The hill leading up from the village was long and steep but well worth the climb. The view to the sea was spectacular from up here, and I walked the final steps backwards just to savour it. The lighthouse, painted

70

in red and white stripes, looked like something from a fairground. Even without its light on, it stood out for miles against the grey rocks and dark sea. But then, I supposed, that was the idea, which was why recently the German pilots had taken a liking to it.

As they often did when I was tired, my thoughts took a funny turn. Perhaps, like the lighthouse, there were people who were meant to stand out, who were made to be noticed and make a difference.

It brought me *slap-bang* to Sukie.

All week I'd savoured doing the delivery round as a time when my brain went blissfully blank. And yet back at Queenie's I'd looked at Sukie's note so many times the paper was wearing thin. It had to be a secret of some sort: why else would it be written in code?

I'd no idea.

My sister had liked raspberry jam on toast, and left long brown hairs in our sink that blocked the plughole. She'd slept late on Saturdays. Turned the wireless up loud when a dance tune came on. But when I thought of her now, it was like there was this whole other Sukie I didn't know, and it frightened me.

Taking a deep breath, I turned away from the sea. Salters Terrace was easy to spot: it was the last row of stone cottages in Budmouth Point. To my surprise – and dismay – standing outside number 4 was Esther Jenkins.

She was leaning against the wall, one leg tucked up behind her. Her face was blotchy like she'd been crying again. I wanted to ask if she was all right, but she looked so awfully fierce, I didn't have the nerve.

'Can you give this to Mrs Drummond, please?' I asked, hating how small I sounded. I held out the parcel of chicken.

'Give it to her yourself,' Esther said flatly. 'The old witch is inside.'

I stared at her, appalled but a little bit impressed. Then I noticed the suitcase on the doorstep, a school blazer and hat slung across it.

'Are you staying here?' I asked.

'Not if I can help it, no.' Snatching up her things, Esther disappeared off down the hill.

Mrs Drummond came to the door almost straight away. I recognised her from the village hall the other night; she was the woman who'd stayed with Esther while she cried.

'That girl is *impossible*!' she sighed, gazing past me into the street. 'Where's she gone? Did you see her?'

'Umm . . . she just went off.' I wasn't sure what else to say. 'Here's your delivery from the shop. And Queenie says can you return yesterday's bacon?'

'Right you are. 'Tis a shame to waste it.' Taking the chicken, she turned to go back inside for the bacon. But something caught her attention and she froze.

'Listen to that,' she said, finger raised. 'Planes.'

I frowned. '*Planes?* What, like *aeroplanes*?'

'German ones, I'll bet you, on their way to bomb poor Plymouth again.'

Mrs Drummond was right. There, on the wind, was the unmistakable drone of aircraft. A familiar dread grew in the pit of my stomach.

'I'd better go,' I said and hurried away, anxious to find Cliff.

LOOSE LIPS
SINK SHIPS

As I ran down the main street, other people were coming out of their houses: women still tying on pinnies, old men in undervests, children rubbing the sleep from their eyes.

I was glad to find Cliff almost immediately, standing with Queenie on the steps of the post office. I tried to hurry him back inside, thinking the cellar would be a good place to shelter.

'Oh give over, Olive!' Cliff cried. 'No one else is going in.'

Incredibly, there was no air-raid warden, nor any sign of one on their way. We might as well have been watching a horse race or a carnival procession for how relaxed everyone seemed. Determined not to leave Cliff on his own, I muttered crossly how foolish it was not to go inside.

Everyone was gazing out to sea. It was a bright winter's day, the sun so low and glarey you had to shield your eyes, yet the dark shapes of the Luftwaffe were clearly visible in the sky.

'If Jerry bombs my cabbages,' said a man with shaving foam still on his cheeks, 'he'll have me to answer to!'

'Oh, Jim,' Mrs Moore who ran the bakery called across the street. 'They're heading for Plymouth, you daft ha'porth, not your garden!'

What bothered me was the planes were getting closer. And louder. There were six of them: one out in front, two flying higher, two directly below, one bringing up the rear. They flew parallel to the coast, close enough to see the distinctive black crosses on the planes' sides. Close enough to be almost level with the long, low platform of rocks on which stood the lighthouse.

'Let's go, Cliff,' I said again.

'In a minute.' He shrugged off my arm. 'This is the cat's bananas!'

'They're German fighter planes – *real* ones,' I said through gritted teeth. 'It's not some film at the Picture Palace.' I didn't like that he'd used Sukie's phrase either, *and* got it wrong.

Someone shouted: 'Look! They're turning inland by the lighthouse!'

Just a few hundred feet above the lighthouse, the German formation was changing shape.

'That bleeding lighthouse,' said old Mr Watkins, whose tobacco ration I delivered every day. 'Them Jerry pilots are using it to find their way. Look at them! Clear as day they are!'

'Not surprised,' Mrs Moore replied. 'It stands out like a beacon.'

I watched in despair as the first plane turned almost at right angles. The others followed close on its tail. It was obvious that they were, like the man said, using the lighthouse to guide them in. Out of the corner of my eye I saw Queenie bend down and pick something up off the ground.

Within moments, the sky above us darkened. Everyone cowered down. I grabbed Cliff and we clung to each other; it was terror on my part, though Cliff was grinning madly.

At little more than roof height, the planes went over. You could see numbers on their undersides. The sections of metal held together with rivets. The stench of burning engine fuel made my throat catch. And the *noise*. It was so horribly high-pitched, I thought my ears would burst.

'Jeez!' Cliff yelled.

I couldn't bear to look any more. It was then I noticed Queenie. She was the only person in the street not cowering. Her arm raised, she was hurling stones at the planes. I don't know if she hit them: it was her face that shocked me more. Glasses askew, teeth bared, she looked almost *savage*.

Once the last plane had gone over, a stunned silence fell. It made the ringing in my ears even worse. Then all at once everyone was talking in that jokey, shrill way people do when they've been scared and are relieved it's over.

Finally, Cliff let me drag him back to the post office where, once inside, we started babbling with nervous excitement.

'If they'd turned their guns on us we'd all be dead.' I snapped my fingers. 'Just like that.'

'It was amazing, Olive.'

'*Terrifying*, more like.'

'The plane was *so* close, wasn't it? Did you see what their pilots did? It was like the lighthouse was a signpost or something, telling them where to turn.'

'Did *you* see what Queenie—' I stopped, reddening.

Queenie had come in so close behind us, I thought she'd overheard. Luckily though she was deep in conversation with Mrs Henderson.

'Ephraim wouldn't take her,' Mrs Henderson was saying. 'He's too busy with the lighthouse.'

'Huh!' Queenie tutted irritably. 'And the rest of us *aren't* busy, I suppose, so it's easy for me to take her?'

I wondered who they were talking about.

'It's probably just his way of saying—'

'— that he doesn't want her finding out before it's all arranged,' Queenie cut in. 'We mustn't get her hopes up.'

It sounded rather mysterious to me.

Mrs Henderson nodded. 'You know how he is, dear. He doesn't get attached to anyone, does he? He'll never marry that one, not after what his father was like when his mother died. Poor Ephraim's seen enough heartbreak to last him a lifetime.'

'We all have,' Queenie retorted. Though she honestly didn't seem heartbroken, not like Mum did. She looked as tough as steel. Then she sighed. 'All right, one more won't make much difference. She can double up with Olive in the attic.' Before I fully realised what was happening there were three people, not two, in front of us. 'Cliff, Olive, you'd better meet our new evacuee.'

It was Esther Jenkins.

'Crikey,' Cliff said under his breath. 'Just our luck.'

My heart sank horribly. We'd been doing all right here with Queenie these past few days. It felt like we were settling in. Now I'd a nasty sense that that was all about to change.

'Why don't you show Esther to your room, Olive dear?' Mrs Henderson suggested.

'I'll take her,' Cliff offered, seeing my face. 'Come on, Esther.'

Sullen and silent, Esther picked up her suitcase. She followed Cliff through the door at the back of the shop that led to the rest of the house.

'Go with them,' Mrs Henderson mouthed, shooing me away.

I shot Queenie a pleading look, but she ignored me. So reluctantly, I did as I was told. As I left Mrs Henderson said something I didn't catch.

'She did *what*?' Queenie gasped.

'Sssh! Not so loud!' Mrs Henderson hissed. 'You're the only house left with any room. I could hardly put her in my goats' shed, could I?'

On the other side of the door, I hesitated before closing it: they were talking about Esther.

'It was probably a misunderstanding,' Mrs Henderson went on. 'Esther swears she explained bacon wasn't kosher – that was why she wouldn't eat it. She wasn't making a fuss for no reason.'

I knew what 'kosher' meant. It was the types of food

a Jewish person could eat, according to their beliefs, which must mean Esther was a Jew.

Queenie breathed in sharply. 'That chicken won't be kosher, either. None of our meat is. Have you spoken to Mrs Drummond?'

I didn't catch the answer. Something was happening upstairs. A door slammed at the top of the house. Then footsteps clattered down the attic stairs, stopped, and went back up again.

'That's my room,' Cliff was saying in a rather pained voice. 'I'm not sharing with a girl.'

By the time I reached the first-floor landing, Cliff was sounding more desperate.

'No, Esther, you can't just take over . . .'

Something bumped across the floor overhead. There was another thud. A laugh.

'Stop it! Those are Olive's!' Cliff cried.

In a rush of anger, I charged up the attic stairs. The cheek of it! She'd only been here five minutes and was already interfering with our things.

Then Esther said, 'Your sister's got a lot of socks.'

My heart stopped.

She was in my sock drawer, where I'd hidden Sukie's note.

'Put that back, it's not yours,' Cliff protested.

Esther laughed. 'Is it a love letter? Has Olive got a sweetheart?'

I stormed into my room. The floor was strewn with clothes – *my* clothes. Esther was in the process of clearing the top two drawers. She'd also moved my books from the windowsill.

'What are you doing?' I cried.

'Making space for my things,' she said as if it were obvious. 'By the way, I found this.'

Between her fingers she twirled Sukie's note. It had been very recently opened.

I licked my lips.

'*Is* it a love letter?' Esther asked again.

'No,' I stammered. 'I . . . I . . . don't think so.'

'Don't you know what it says?' She was surprised. 'So it's a secret code? Isn't that a bit *dangerous*?'

I wiped my palms on my skirt: I knew what she was implying, and took a step towards her.

'Are you calling my sister a *spy*?'

Esther Jenkins slowly smiled. 'I don't think I mentioned a *sister*, did I?'

I realised then what I'd done: I'd put my size five foot right in it.

ATTACK ON ALL FRONTS

I tried to keep calm. 'Look, you can have the sock drawer, I don't mind. Just give me back the note and we'll call it quits.'

But Esther wasn't stupid. She could see how much I wanted that piece of paper, and kept hold of it.

'Sukie's not a spy! What're you talking about?' Cliff glanced at me, bewildered.

'Of course she's not,' I reassured him.

'So why's Olive gone red?' Esther asked.

'Have not!' Though I could feel the heat in my cheeks all too well.

Esther was looking at me very intently now. 'What *is* your sister up to?'

She sounded almost concerned. It threw me into total panic. As I made a grab for the note, she hid it behind her back. 'Hey! It's rude to snatch!'

Something snapped in me, then. I'd never pulled a person by the hair before. I didn't know it made a ripping sound. A look of surprise flashed across Esther's face.

'You little cow!' she yelped.

Then it was all fists and feet, and we both fell to the floor.

'I never liked you from the start,' Esther spat, her plaits dangling in my face.

'Same goes for you, with bells on,' I retorted.

She walloped my jaw so hard I felt it creak. I tried to roll sideways but couldn't move for her weight.

'Get off her! Let go!' yelled Cliff. He was behind Esther now, tugging at her coat.

'Keep back!' I warned him.

It was too late. Esther's elbow swung backwards. It hit Cliff in the face with a meaty thud. Immediately, there was blood on his top lip; within seconds it was dripping down his chin on to his jumper.

'For crying out loud!' I gasped.

As Esther twisted round to see what she'd done, I managed to wriggle free and grab Cliff. I steered him towards the bedroom door.

'Find Queenie,' I told him. 'Keep your hand pressed to your lip.'

Esther stood up awkwardly. 'Look, I shouldn't have—'

'Don't you ever,' I cut across her, so angry I shook, 'EVER touch my brother again.'

There was a thin trail of blood all the way down the stairs. In the hallway, the open cellar door and the hum of voices indicated where Cliff had found Queenie.

'It's not as bad as it looks,' Queenie was saying. 'The bleeding's almost stopped.'

Relieved, I paused on the bottom step, taking a few deep breaths to calm down. I'd never lost my temper like that before – I didn't even know I *had* all that anger inside me. It was a bit frightening, to be honest.

'Olive?'

I turned round. Esther was at the top of the stairs. 'You're not going to tell Queenie, are you? I didn't mean to hit him.'

'Just give me back the note,' I demanded.

Esther folded her arms. 'I haven't got it.'

She was lying. The sound of Cliff crying distracted me, though. Leaving Esther on the stairs, I headed for the cellar.

'That's right,' Esther called out. 'Run to the grown-ups.' And she said something else in another language: it didn't sound very polite.

I was already halfway down the cellar steps when Queenie appeared at the bottom. Lit by an oil lamp, the place was shadowy and smelled of damp. I wondered why she spent so much time down here.

'Is he all right?' I asked anxiously, looking over her shoulder to where Cliff sat in a chair, his head tipped back to slow the bleeding.

Queenie wouldn't let me pass. There was a smear of blood on her cheek, which made her look rather terrifying.

'What on earth is going on – IN MY HOUSE?' she thundered.

I flinched. For a little person, she had a very loud voice.

'Well?' Queenie asked. 'Is someone going to tell me what this is all about?'

Cliff had stopped crying – the shock, probably. Behind me, I heard the door creak. Turning my head slightly I saw Esther – or rather, the scuffed toes of her shoes – on the cellar steps.

No one spoke. Not for a very long, loaded time.

'Right.' Queenie tutted impatiently. 'Esther, go and wait in the kitchen. I'll deal with you in a moment.'

'Why me?' Esther cried. 'I didn't start it.'

'Just do as you're told!' Queenie roared.

I jumped. It had the desired effect on Esther too, who stormed back up the stairs, slamming the cellar door so hard the whole room seemed to shake.

'Oh!' Queenie breathed in sharply. She was staring at the far end of the cellar now, where a clock hung precariously on the wall. Like the one upstairs in the shop, it wasn't working. Even more peculiar was the time it'd stopped – ten past two – was exactly the same. It couldn't be a coincidence, surely.

'Don't move,' Queenie ordered.

I didn't, though the clock had other plans. As the plaster crumbled, the clock slid almost gracefully down the wall. When it hit the floor it made all sorts of tinkling noises. Bits from its insides were now on the outside – brass springs, a chain, a funny little screw. It was horrible, like a bird after a cat's had it. I remembered what Mrs Henderson said last night about Queenie's clocks: there was nothing faintly *romantic* about this one.

'Wasn't working anyway,' Cliff muttered. I told him to *shhh*.

By now I'd noticed the rest of the room. Mostly it was just dusty shelves and boxes, with a bare brick floor that sloped down towards the middle. Stood over this was a huge, square table, which was covered in notes – handwritten, scribbled ones, done on little scraps of paper and weighed down by a huge grey pebble. There were also maps, a compass and an old brass pocket watch that *did* seem to be ticking.

Intrigued, I shuffled a bit closer to the table. Queenie must've seen me looking, for she straightened up from inspecting her clock and was suddenly in front of me, blocking my view.

'Back upstairs, you two,' she said briskly. 'There are things down here not meant for children's eyes.'

I didn't move.

'It was about Sukie,' I said in a rush. 'The argument with Esther, I mean. She was trying to make out that my sister was up to something . . . well . . . *suspicious*.'

I watched Queenie's face for a sign. A clue. There was nothing.

'Is she?' I asked. 'Is that why she disappeared? Is something going on? I've been trying to ask you for ages and you just won't say.'

'There's nothing *to* say, Olive.' Queenie sounded annoyed. 'Even if there was I couldn't tell you. There's a war on, you know, and careless talk costs lives.'

'But I thought . . .'

'Then don't *think*,' she snapped. 'Go upstairs and get your things, both of you.'

'I didn't mean to—'

She interrupted: 'It's easier to move you two on than Esther, believe me.'

I stared at her in disbelief: was she throwing us out?

'That's not fair!' I cried. 'You took us in first. You promised Gloria you'd have us!'

Queenie sighed. 'Sometimes sisters have to break their promises to each other. I'm sorry, but there we are.'

She looked at me like she expected me to understand, but I didn't.

*

Half an hour later Queenie was marching us down the hill towards the harbour. I was still angry that we'd had to leave. Cliff's lip wasn't great, either; it'd swelled up and made him look like a duck. I was pretty certain Queenie knew more about Sukie than she was letting on, which made moving out even more rotten. We couldn't honestly live happily under the same roof as Esther though, that was clear.

'Where are we going?' I asked grumpily. Carrying Cliff's case as well as mine, I hoped it wasn't far.

'You'll see.' Arms hovering at our backs like a bossy mother hen, she steered us on down the street past knots of people. Eyes slid over us as we went by.

'That's the thanks you get from taking in strangers,' someone muttered.

'Aye,' another voice agreed. 'They don't teach 'em manners in London, do they?'

'Ignore them,' I said to Cliff. With suitcases bumping painfully against my shins, I was trying very hard not to cry.

'I still don't see why it was us who had to go,' Cliff moaned.

'Mrs Henderson said no one else would take Esther in – I heard her say it,' I informed him.

'You shouldn't be listening in on other people's conversations, Olive,' said Queenie.

'But we're Sukie's brother and sister,' I protested. 'You're supposed to be her friend!'

Queenie looked surprised. 'Me? I don't know what you mean.'

'You've written to . . .' I trailed off hopelessly. There was no point in arguing any more. Queenie had made up her mind.

'Well, I don't trust Esther Jenkins,' I muttered, as much to myself as anyone. 'And I bet she'll not be as quick doing the deliveries, either.'

Queenie gave me a withering look. 'For your information, Esther's moved house, city and country more times than you've had hot dinners. I don't think she'd manage it again. At least you two have each other.'

Glancing at Cliff, all I felt was *more* worry, not less. I hadn't got the hang of this 'big sister' lark – you only had to look at Cliff's split lip to see my attempt at looking after him wasn't exactly going well.

'All Esther's anger, all that bluster – it's just a front,' Queenie went on. 'Behind it she's a smashing girl. You need to give her a chance.'

'She said horrible things about my sister!' I insisted, though I was beginning to feel uncomfortable. Because I'd started the fight, hadn't I? I'd been the angry one – Esther had almost tried to apologise.

Queenie stopped. 'You've heard of the Kindertransport, have you?'

'Some Jewish kids joined our school from Europe,' I said. 'But I don't see what—'

'Esther was one of them,' Queenie interrupted. 'Not at your school but another one in London. She's a Jewish refugee.'

'Well, she as good as called Sukie a spy!' I pointed out.

Queenie ignored my comment. 'Esther's had a terrible time of it. Everyone she loves has either died or disappeared, or, failing that, lives in another country. Imagine what that feels like, can you?'

I swallowed miserably. The thing was I *could* imagine it – bits of it, anyway – and I felt ashamed, which didn't improve my temper.

'That doesn't excuse what she did to Cliff's lip,' I mumbled, though really I was cross with myself. After what I'd overheard about kosher meat, I should have realised she was a Kindertransport child. But I didn't think, did I? Instead, I'd grabbed her by the hair.

What sort of person was I turning into to be so bitter? So angry?

Queenie set off walking again. 'That lip'll heal in no time. Now hurry up and stop dawdling.'

Glancing sideways at Cliff, I felt a funny sensation in my chest. His lip looked horrid now but he would recover – Queenie was right. At least he was here, my living, breathing, sticky-handed brother. I was pretty lucky, all things considered.

By now we'd almost reached the sea. To our left was the beach, steep with shingle. A few hundred yards away, beyond the last groyne, the shingle became sand that looked flat and wet, and there was a sign that said 'Danger! Quicksand!' except the word 'sand' had worn away. It was a bleak, uninviting place; I bet it did swallow people whole, like Queenie said. You certainly wouldn't need telling twice to keep away.

To the right was the harbour. The tide was out this afternoon leaving the few boats that were there sitting lopsided on the sand. At the very end of the sea wall was the lighthouse and though I was still feeling miserable, I couldn't help but think how magnificent it looked. The wall connecting it to the mainland reminded me of a cobbled street. Heading towards us along it was a person with a smallish white dog nipping about at their heels.

Queenie stopped, raising her arm to wave. The person – a man – paused, then waved back. He was dressed from head to toe in black oilskins that made him look sleek and enormous like a whale.

'Who's *that*?' Cliff asked eagerly, though I think he meant the dog.

'Ephraim Pengilly,' Queenie answered, 'the lighthouse keeper. He doesn't know it yet, but he's about to take you both in. Whether he likes it or not.'

CARELESS TALK COSTS LIVES

Queenie introduced us by slapping our ration book down into Ephraim's hand. 'Your evacuees. *This* is the war effort too, you know.'

The lighthouse keeper's dog took a sniff of Queenie's shoes and growled. It was probably a good judge of character, I decided. Yet as my brain caught up with what was happening, I realised life had taken a sudden turn for the better. Putting down our suitcases, I gave Cliff's arm an excited squeeze. We were going to live in the lighthouse!

Ephraim, though, was confused. 'Hold on a—'

'You might've convinced Mrs Henderson that you couldn't have Esther Jenkins,' Queenie spoke over him. 'But the situation's changed.' Turning on her heel, she strode back up the street, leaving us on the harbourside.

Ephraim studied us in disbelief as if we'd been magicked out of thin air. He was nothing like I expected a lighthouse keeper to be. Instead of a jolly-looking, bushy-bearded old man, he was young – about Sukie's age and, unlike Queenie, actually looked it. He had pale blue eyes, dark ruffled hair. And his face, not much given to smiling, made me rather like him. He wasn't remotely whale-sized, either; it was only the oilskins that were huge.

I remembered what Mrs Henderson had said about him preferring to live alone, though that wasn't why Esther couldn't stay here. It seemed to be to do with a plan they didn't want her to know about. As it was, Ephraim seemed unsure what to do with us too, or what to say, though his dog happily set about licking Cliff's knees.

'He's smashing!' grinned Cliff, smoothing the dog's head. 'What's his name?'

'Pixie. It's a *she*.' Ephraim frowned. 'She doesn't usually like strangers, but she's taken to you.' Which seemed to convince him we were all right; with a big sigh, he picked up our suitcases.

'Come on, then. We'd best get moving before the tide comes in.' Whistling to Pixie, Ephraim set off back towards the lighthouse.

'Is he talking to us or the dog?' Cliff asked me.

'Us, you ninny.' I gave him a playful nudge. 'Are you okay? Really?'

'Honestly, Olive, stop fussing. I'm fine.'

I had to admit he looked happier than I'd seen him in days.

Picking our way over the slippery cobbles, we followed Ephraim. The road out to the lighthouse was set so high it felt like walking along the top of a very wide wall. A drop of about fifteen feet separated us from the beach below. From up here the wind, blowing off the sea, felt mean even by Budmouth Point's standards. It blew straight through Mum's smart coat and I quickly found myself wishing for my old one that didn't fit but at least kept out the chill.

After a hundred yards or so the road stopped at steps which led to the lighthouse. The front door was about twenty feet up and reached by a rusty iron ladder set into the building itself. If there was a downside to living in the lighthouse then this was it: just the sight of the ladder made me distinctly queasy, though I knew it'd be even worse for Cliff.

Ephraim was waiting at the bottom of the steps.

'The dog goes up first,' he explained.

'The *dog*?' I frowned. 'Don't you carry her?'

As Pixie yapped and spun in circles at Ephraim's feet, it dawned on me she'd done this before, many times.

'Up, girl, up!' he cried.

She hopped on to the ladder, front paws on the nearest rung, hind paws on the one below. On she went, up and up and up. It wasn't exactly graceful – she sort of stepped, sort of climbed. It was heart-in-mouth stuff to watch. On reaching the top, she pushed open the front door with her snout, then sat inside, looking down at us.

'That's incredible!' Cliff cried, though he was beginning to look a bit sick.

'Amazing,' I agreed, forcing myself to smile.

Next it was the suitcases' turn. Hoisting mine on to his shoulder, Ephraim went up the ladder. Just watching made my mouth go dry. Pushing my case inside the front door, he came back down for Cliff's.

'Once I'm at the top you follow, got it?' he said to me, settling the second suitcase on his shoulder.

I nodded anxiously. Cliff was jiggling his leg like he always did when he was nervous.

'Deep breaths,' I told him. 'Be brave.'

He gulped. 'Can I go first and get it over with?'

'All right.'

'Come up behind him,' Ephraim yelled to me. 'Don't hang about.'

I'd noticed how the beach on either side of us was already underwater. Though looking up wasn't any more comforting: from this angle the iron ladder seemed steeper and more precarious. Squaring his shoulders, Cliff placed his hands on the lowest rung. When he'd climbed far enough, I got on behind.

The higher we went, the stronger the wind became. It didn't help that the ladder felt greasy with sea spray, making it hard to get a firm grip; harder still to stop your feet slipping forwards. Beneath my coat, I began to sweat.

There were only a few rungs left now. Beyond Cliff, I saw the ledge of the front door, its red paint peeling. Just inside, quivering excitedly, was Pixie.

Above me Cliff stopped. His ankles were shaking badly.

'Keep going! We're nearly there!' I called.

But he seemed to be stuck.

'Cliff,' I said slowly. 'Nod if you can hear me.'

He gave a tiny nod.

'Good. Now lift your left foot up.'

He did it. I breathed in relief.

'Brilliant. Now do the same with your right.'

And he *did* do the same, but the ladder was too slippery. In panic, he grabbed the sides of the ladder. His feet kicked in the space above my head.

'Find the ladder!' I screamed. 'Put your feet back on the ladder!'

Yet the more he kicked, the more he missed the rung. 'The ladder, Cliff! It's there, just to your left!'

Don't let go, I begged. Only now his hands were slipping down too. Any second he'd come crashing into me, and I didn't think I could catch him.

Then, just like that, his feet lifted up. He wasn't above my head any more: Ephraim was, his arms working madly to haul my limp brother in through the door. Within moments, I was inside too. I flopped down beside Cliff, too weak to fend off Pixie's muzzle as it nudged under my arm.

When I managed to sit up, I saw a room with curved walls and a staircase in the middle that twirled upwards. Hung about the place were fishing nets and fat coils of rope, and slumped against one such pile was Cliff, looking terribly relieved. On my hands and knees, I crawled over to him.

'You're going to have to practise that ladder,' I told him, getting my breath back. 'My heart won't stand it otherwise.'

Cliff smiled, not at me, but up at Ephraim, who was peeling off his wet oilskins. 'You saved my life.'

''Tis only a ladder,' Ephraim muttered shyly. 'No one's ever fallen off, not even the dog.'

I wasn't sure I believed him, swallowing the lump in

my throat. 'Well, thanks awfully anyway.'

I think he blushed. 'Right,' he said, moving on quickly, 'let's get you both settled in.'

Passing us our suitcases, he hurried up the stairs. My legs still felt shaky; Cliff, though, bounded eagerly ahead. On the next floor, Ephraim unlatched an old-looking door.

'This is where you'll sleep,' Ephraim said, pushing it open.

'Gosh!' I gasped. 'I mean … wow!'

It was perhaps the nicest room I'd ever seen. For one thing, there was so much light. I counted at least six windows – little ones, arched at the top and set deep into the walls. Everything was painted white, even the floor. On either side of the room two beds hugged the curved lighthouse walls. Above each was a shelf of books from which hung beautiful, sea-blue lanterns. I didn't even mind having to share the room with Cliff. The beds weren't made up, so I asked where the blankets and pillows were kept.

'I'll do that after I've shown you the rest,' said Ephraim, heading back to the stairs. He seemed to be in a bit of a rush.

Leaving our suitcases unpacked, we followed him to the next floor, which was where Ephraim slept.

The level above that was a sitting room with a kitchen. Again, it was another light-filled room with rugs on the floor and cushions on the chairs in colours that didn't match. There were saucepans hanging from hooks, plates stacked on shelves. Log baskets. Old newspapers. Balls of wool where someone had been knitting what looked like socks. Mum would've said the place needed a jolly good tidy, but to me it was a nice kind of mess.

'Where's the actual "light" of the lighthouse?' I asked.

Ephraim pointed to the ceiling. 'The control room's at the top. That's where I work.'

'What do you do – being a lighthouse keeper, I mean?'

'Give guidance to ships as they pass by, look out for problems, ships in difficulty, that sort of thing. I have to record everything that happens in my log book – weather, traffic, who I speak to, what I see. It's the law. Oh, and I keep the equipment in good order too.'

It sounded an awful lot of work for one person.

'Is the light on now?' Cliff wanted to know.

Ephraim shook his head. 'Only at night and in bad weather. There are rocks on this part of the coast that could easily snag the bottom of a boat. And the quicksands – you wouldn't want to get caught in those.'

'Queenie told us,' Cliff said enthusiastically. 'Has anyone ever *died* there?'

'Well...' Ephraim took a deep breath. 'Not recently, which is one reason why the light is so important.'

It was obvious how much he cared for the lighthouse: it was by far the most he'd said to us all in one go.

'Miss Carter says there're plans to turn off the light, but how'll that help if the Germans are flying over in daylight?' I asked, a bit baffled.

Ephraim's face darkened. 'It's just gossip. You can't not have a lighthouse at Budmouth. It's too dangerous.'

I thought German bombs were pretty risky too, though judging by the look on Ephraim's face I thought it best not to say so.

*

He didn't speak much after that. Nor did he offer to show us the top floor. Yet, unlike Queenie, he realised that children ate and drank. Setting the table with cups and plates, he made us tea and toast, which we spread with a funny pink jam that he told us was made from crab apples.

'Do they come from the sea?' asked Cliff, so seriously it made me snort. I don't think Ephraim got the joke.

'Your lip needs cleaning,' he said to Cliff after we'd eaten. With water from the kettle, he wiped the blood off my brother's face, and much to Cliff's disappointment said he didn't need stitches.

Getting up from the table, I began to collect our plates. It was best to start as we meant to go on and show Ephraim that we could look after ourselves. As lighthouse keeper he had enough to do already.

Ephraim leaped to his feet. 'Leave the dishes!'

'Oh.' I put the plates down. 'Shall I make up our beds, then? If you show me where the blankets are—'

'I'll do that too,' he said.

Confused, I sat down again.

I tried to explain: 'At Queenie's I did her deliveries, and Cliff worked—'

'There's nothing for you to help with here,' Ephraim interrupted sharply.

Now I was embarrassed. 'Sorry. I didn't mean to—'

'Just don't go touching anything that's not yours, all right?'

'None of it's ours,' Cliff replied. 'So how can we?'

It was a fair point. All I'd meant was that he should let us muck in. The jobs at Queenie's made us feel like we were contributing.

Yet Ephraim was firm. 'You're both welcome here but those are my rules. No snooping in cupboards, no listening in on conversations or going up to the lighthouse control room, got it?'

'Because there's a war on,' I muttered, thinking of what Queenie'd said. 'And careless talk costs lives.'

I'd heard that line a bit too often today: it was beginning to sound like an excuse. Queenie, I was sure, was up to something in her cellar, something secret we weren't allowed to know about.

And what was the real reason why Esther couldn't stay here? Something to do with not getting her hopes up, that's what Mrs Henderson had said. I glanced at Ephraim, at his closed face, and wondered if he was hiding things too.

WALLS HAVE EARS

That night I lay awake in my unfamiliar bed. Every few minutes when the lighthouse beam turned, the brightness was so strong it came through the blackout curtains, catching the surface of my seashell and making me think of Dad.

The last time he'd been home on leave, I'd found him out in our yard staring at the coal shed. Beckoning me over, he gave me a leg up and told me to look at the bird. It was a pigeon, lying amongst the old leaves. It didn't look like the normal, greasy-feathered kind: this one was a lovely grey colour with white around its neck.

'It's not moving,' I said.

'The poor thing's dead,' Dad explained. 'From exhaustion, I expect.'

'Or from Gloria's cat. It got two blackbirds and a mouse last week,' I told him.

Dad pointed to the bird's left leg, which stuck out

stiff as a twig from its body. 'See that metal cylinder?'

Craning my neck I could just about see what looked like one of Sukie's lipsticks tied on to the bird.

'This pigeon's probably flown all the way from Europe. There'll be a message inside, something important from the front line.' He told me that's what pigeons were being used for nowadays – to send messages from places where the post couldn't reach.

'Can we open it?' I asked.

'Of course not!' Dad sounded horrified and put me down on the ground. 'That message will be top secret, Olive. We need to hand it over to the authorities as quickly as we can.'

I couldn't remember what happened next. A call to the Ministry of Defence, I supposed, or the police. What stuck with me was the sight of that dead bird. It must've flown over France, over the English Channel, reaching us just as its little pigeon heart gave out. After all that effort the least we could've done was read the message. It seemed so important that we did.

It felt a bit like that with Sukie's note. Not being able to read it was so frustrating. We still didn't know anything about her whereabouts, not even if she was dead or alive. We didn't have the note any more, either – Esther did.

'Olive?' Cliff was awake.

'Go back to sleep.' I turned over to face the wall.

'Can't. I need to tell you something.'

Sighing, I rolled over again to see Cliff out of bed and crossing the room towards me. Lifting up the bedclothes, he slipped in beside me, warm as toast and not in the slightest bit sleepy.

'I got it back off Esther,' he whispered, pushing a piece of paper into my hand. 'Just before she elbowed me, I snatched it from her pocket.'

It was Sukie's note.

'Thanks awfully!' I cried, ruffling Cliff's hair. 'You're brilliant, you are.'

So Esther hadn't been lying when she said she didn't have it, because by then Cliff had already got it back. I was thrilled to have it again.

'Olive.' Cliff's tone was so serious suddenly, my stomach tightened. 'D'you think Esther was right?'

'About what?' I asked warily.

But I knew what he meant: he'd read the note again – or tried to; the code made it impossible. He was wondering if his sister was a spy. I didn't blame him. She was, after all, the bravest, cleverest person I knew. If anyone could outwit the Germans, I'd put my pocket money on it being Sukie. In the books I'd read, though, spies worked alone, whereas Sukie had lots of friends – people from her schooldays, people at work. She had a penpal too, who she'd written to every night, though I was beginning to wonder how much of the 'pal' part Queenie really was.

I breathed deeply. 'I don't think she's a spy. I don't reckon she went missing in the air raid, either.'

Cliff was quiet as he took it in. 'Where is she, then?'

I thought about the man she'd met; the foreign map at home in her drawer. About what I'd tried to see on Queenie's table earlier, and Ephraim's strict house rules.

'I don't know,' I said carefully. '*Yet.*'

All these things might be random clues. Or . . . they might somehow link together. As we lay there, side by side, I could almost feel the certainty growing in my mind. Ephraim *and* Queenie were hiding things from us. And Sukie definitely wasn't the sort to work alone.

*

The next morning, in the bright light of day, the code looked so simple.

```
DAY 9
I  26  8  T/U  I
J  26  9  16  19  12  6  8  I
B  26  T  -  50.26
B  12  13  20  +  3.6
```

Yet whichever way I read it – back to front, upside down, top to bottom – I couldn't work out what it meant.

'I give up!' I groaned. We were in the sitting room part of the lighthouse, the table still full of dirty breakfast things which we didn't dare wash up.

'Day 9 – that's easy. It means in nine days' time,' said Cliff. I got the sense he wasn't giving it his full attention, not with Pixie at his feet begging toast crumbs.

'Very good, clever clogs. Starting from when?'

He shrugged. 'The night at the cinema?'

It was possible. Or it could be nine o'clock in the morning. Or an unknown date in the past, or future. There were so many different meanings – and we were only on the first line.

Exasperated, I flopped into the nearest chair. Maybe codes were a bit like crosswords: the more you stared at them, the harder they got to solve. Putting the note in my skirt pocket, I decided to give my brain a break from it. Pixie, by now, had got bored and fallen asleep, and

Cliff was gazing out of the window through a pair of binoculars. The room was quiet. From this particular seat near the stairs, I discovered I could hear Ephraim at work in the control room above us.

The crackles and beeps told me he was talking on a radio. He'd say things like 'squalls' and 'riptides', 'knots' and 'co-ordinates' which sounded impressive, though I didn't know what they meant. The other noise was a familiar *click-clack* sound that went on long after the radio conversation was over. Yesterday, I'd seen balls of wool here on the chair. A half-finished sock. Needles.

Ephraim was knitting, by the sounds of it, very fast.

'So?' said Cliff, when I told him to listen. He turned from the window to look at me through the binoculars. It was rather disconcerting. 'Everyone knits, don't they?'

Certainly Mum and Gloria did – they made socks for our troops, but only a few pairs each. Usually it was around Christmas time, and they'd parcel them up with chocolate bars and pipe tobacco to send off to a British Forces address somewhere abroad.

It wasn't Christmas now, though, and yet upstairs Ephraim sounded like he was going for a knitting world record. Whoever he was making all these socks for clearly had very cold feet. Or needed warm clothes in a hurry.

FREEDOM IS IN PERIL

The following Monday afternoon we started lessons at the village school. It'd taken a bit of arranging because there was only one classroom, which we couldn't all fit in, so the Budmouth Point kids were to have their lessons in the morning. You'd have thought they'd be thrilled to be knocking off school early. But, I was taken aback to find a group of them at the entrance when we arrived.

'Sssh! They're coming!' someone said in a very loud whisper.

In that moment I wished with all my heart I was back in London going to St Thomas's as usual, walking through the gates with Maggie and Susan. In Mum's smart coat I felt suddenly self-conscious, unsure whether to stop or hurry past. Yet compared to the lighthouse ladder which we'd had to climb down to get here, for Cliff this was the easy part.

'Hullo,' he said to the local kids, squinting from

under his school cap. 'I'm Cliff.'

'Are you any good at football?' one of the younger boys asked.

'I can play a bit,' Cliff admitted.

Another boy, with a missing front tooth, said to me: 'I've seen you before in the village. You're the delivery girl, aren't you?'

'I was,' I replied. 'We're living at the lighthouse now.'

'Magic!' He whistled. 'What's it like inside? Does he actually talk to you, Mr Pengilly? My mum says he's always sad and never speaks to anyone.'

'He's all right.' I think the boy wanted juicy details but I already felt rather loyal towards Ephraim, whose serious nature struck a chord with me. Anyway, the boy's attention quickly moved on as more evacuees arrived at the gates.

'Are you from London?' a freckle-faced girl asked me. I nodded. Smiled.

'My dad says never mind the Germans, it's them Londoners what's invaded us,' an older boy remarked.

I hoped he might be joking: he certainly had a big grin on his face. Then his mate joined in with 'Send 'em all home. We don't want 'em here.'

And I realised then it wasn't a pleasant grin. Reaching for Cliff's hand, I thought it best to move on into the playground where I could see Mr Barrowman talking to Miss Carter. Glancing behind, I saw the grinning boy's new target was Esther Jenkins, who, like the rest of us, was wearing the uniform of her London school.

'Been frightening the cows in that outfit, have you?' the boy called out.

Esther stopped level with the Budmouth kids. 'Which one of you said that?'

I couldn't help but admire her courage. I'd not seen her since we'd left Queenie's on Friday, and still felt I'd behaved rather shoddily, especially now I knew a bit more about her background. I'd decided to try harder at being friendly next time we met. Watching her now, though, she still seemed full of fight. I wasn't confident my plan would work.

'Are you talking to me?' Esther asked, homing in on the boy with the grin. 'We're guests here, you know. Is *this* how you welcome us?'

Chin up, plaits tossed over her shoulders, she more than stood her ground. The boy, on the other hand, had gone decidedly blotchy.

'That in't a London accent,' he laughed nervously. 'You sound foreign, you do.'

I caught my breath. There was going to be trouble.

I could see Esther's fists clenching by her sides.

Thankfully, Mr Barrowman started ringing the school bell with a huge swing of his arm. Deafening though it was, the noise broke up the group.

We were ushered into a cloakroom to hang our coats and gas masks on hooks bearing other people's names. It was odd being back in a classroom. The rows of desks were familiar enough, as were the books with crumbling spines stacked on the shelves at the back. The smell – chalk dust and floor polish – made me remember none too enthusiastically the equations and algebra that my old teacher Miss Higgins had tried to drum into me without much success.

Though there were only twenty-five of us in our class, we were all ages and sizes, wearing the uniforms of at least four different London schools. One of these was Mr Barrowman's own school, I remembered from the train. He'd been evacuated here with his remaining students, and now faced the challenge of teaching us, though if he was nervous, he didn't show it.

'Robertson!' he barked at an unsuspecting boy. 'Tuck that shirt in. It's not a petticoat!'

Miss Carter was more welcoming, remembering all our names as we shuffled through the classroom door.

'Hullo, everyone, yes, that's right, I'm here as an extra

pair of hands,' she said to us. 'Come in, take a seat.'

As I went by she took me aside. 'Queenie told me about you and Esther falling out. How about you make a fresh start today?'

'Um . . .' I bit my lip nervously. 'I'll try.'

'Good girl.' Miss Carter smiled. 'Look, there's a spare desk next to Esther. Why don't you sit there?'

To be honest, I didn't think Esther would want me sitting near her, and I'd have rather tried to make friends at my own speed. But I liked Miss Carter: she wore bright lipstick and the sort of trousers Sukie called 'slacks', and I knew she meant well.

'Okay,' I agreed.

Esther looked surprised when I sat down next to her, though I wasn't sure how long I'd be there as Mr Barrowman was now busily rearranging everyone's places.

'Younger pupils sit here,' he said, clicking his fingers at the front desks. 'Older pupils take the outside seat in each row.'

I supposed it meant the bigger kids could help the younger ones. In the end neither Esther nor I had to move, since she was a year or so older than me.

'Looks like I'll be helping you, then,' Esther said coolly. 'Please tell me you're not awful at maths.'

'I'm not very *good* at it,' I confessed.

She sat back in her seat with a sigh. 'Typical.'

'SILENCE!' Mr Barrowman's roar made me jump. 'I don't recall inviting this class to talk!'

A hush fell over the room. No one dared speak again, at least not until asked. For me, that dreadful prospect came all too quickly, when, after exercise books were handed out, Mr Barrowman announced we'd be writing in ink.

'No chalk slates or pencils in my class. From now on, you'll all be using dip pens and ink.'

Glancing round, Cliff caught my eye, and we shared an excited look. Writing in ink was what you did in your final year of school at St Thomas's. I'd had a go for fun once and made a frightful mess, but when I'd got the hang of it my handwriting had looked awfully smart.

A boy called David from Mr Barrowman's own school was told to hand out pens. Miss Carter passed around bits of blotting paper. Then Mr Barrowman's stern gaze came to rest on me: 'Olivia, you'll be our class ink monitor for this term.'

I cringed. Everyone knew the job of ink monitor was as good as having 'teacher's pet' stamped on your forehead.

'It's *Olive*, sir,' I mumbled, knowing I'd gone red. 'Do I have to? I'm not very good at pouring.'

He looked at me with such scorn I knew I had no choice. Reluctantly I went to the front to collect the ink can.

'Fill every pupil's inkwell,' Mr Barrowman instructed, handing the can to me. 'Quickly now.'

Each desk had a porcelain cup set in the top left-hand corner for ink. Those on the front row I filled easily enough. But the bigger kids didn't move aside for me so I was stepping over outstretched feet and weaving around their chairs. Their pens, handed out efficiently by David, hovered impatiently over their open books.

'Are we to wait FOR EVER for our ink?' Mr Barrowman cried from the front. 'Hurry UP, girl!'

Hot and bothered, I rushed to the back row. Esther tucked her feet in so I could get closer to her desk.

'Thanks,' I whispered gratefully.

Yet just as I leaned in to pour the ink, a noise from outside made me freeze.

The droning got louder. It was, unmistakably, the sound of aeroplanes – bombers, to be precise. Everyone was looking skywards now. When I saw Miss Carter take off her glasses and slip them in her trouser pocket,

I felt a cold squirm of fear. No one with any sense kept their glasses on during an air raid. It was one thing the London bombings had taught us.

'Do NOT panic,' Mr Barrowman demanded, though when he looked out of the window, he breathed in sharply. 'Heavens above! It's the . . .'

The planes overhead drowned out the rest.

Despite the teacher's orders, I did start to panic. Breathe, I told myself. It's not like last time. You're not alone or out in the street. You're safe. My body remembered it, though. I began to shake, my heart racing so fast I thought I was going to faint.

Whump.

The explosion threw me against Esther's desk. People fell from their chairs. Books tumbled off the shelves. I stayed on the floor, arms wrapped around my head. Beneath me the ground shuddered, and the windows made a popping, crunching sound as their glass cracked.

Silence followed. For a moment, no one moved as the shock sank in. Then, clambering over the upturned chairs, I rushed to Cliff.

'Are you all right?' I cried, brushing the dust from his face.

He nodded, smiling weakly. 'That was terrific!' As

I helped him to his feet, I didn't tell him he looked completely terrified.

Other people were standing up now, dusting down their clothes and checking themselves for cuts or bruises. My ears felt strange but nothing hurt. Beat by beat, my heart began to slow.

'It was a stray bomb. Nothing to fuss about. It's all over now,' Mr Barrowman insisted, ordering us back to our seats. He resumed the lesson where he'd left off, telling us to copy the date into our books, yet when he addressed us there was definitely a tremble in his voice.

Picking up my pen, I realised I was the only one still without ink. I glanced round for my ink can. It was on the floor where I'd dropped it, ink splatted against the wall and up the legs of Esther's desk. As I was working up the courage to tell Mr Barrowman, Esther suddenly cried out, 'I'm bleeding!'

I dropped my pen in alarm. Her hands were covering her face. She was on her feet, staggering backwards so her chair tipped over. Miss Carter rushed over with a hankie.

It wasn't blood: I could see the colour through her hands and it was blue, not red. The ink had got her too, a great wet splat of it right across her forehead.

It wasn't long before the other kids cottoned on. Laughter rippled round the room. Esther, wiping her face in Miss Carter's hankie, realised too. She looked very relieved, and managed a little half-smile. Then as her eye caught mine the smile vanished.

'Not funny,' she mouthed, as if I'd done it on purpose.

*

There was no back-to-normal after that, though Mr Barrowman tried. In the end we were all sent home again.

'Esther, wait!' I cried, as she rushed out of the door before I'd even got my coat on.

'Let her cool down,' Miss Carter advised. 'You look a bit shaken up yourself, Olive. Go home and have a cup of tea.'

I hadn't meant to spill the ink, it was an accident – anyone could see that. The trouble was, with Esther and me things were already spiky and complicated, and the ink spill had made things worse.

'Wow, you look miserable,' Cliff said helpfully as we left school. But that was all he said, guessing I didn't want to talk. We walked out through the school gates in silence.

The stray bomb had come down just beyond the church. No houses had been struck, thankfully; it had landed in someone's front garden. All that was left of it now was a gaping, smoking hole and the remains of a gate. Seeing it made me go panicky again, so we hurried past.

We didn't get much further. Out on the main street, the crowd was so thick it was impossible to squeeze through. Someone had arrived in a motor vehicle, and was obviously so important people had come out of their houses to greet him.

'Who's he?' Cliff asked, standing on tiptoes for a better look.

The man's dark blue coat and peaked cap seemed to be a uniform of sorts.

'Well, he's not the Home Guard or the army,' I deduced.

Then someone shouted, 'The coastguard's here!' and, 'Hurrah for Mr Spratt! He'll sort Jerry out!' until the man was almost swamped by pats on the back. Climbing the nearest front steps, which happened to be Queenie's, he stood, feet apart, to address the crowd. Though not very tall he was broad in the body, which made him look rather square. He seemed to be enjoying all the attention too, puffing out his chest like he'd just won a medal.

'Once again today we find ourselves in this unacceptable situation. Twice this last week German bombers have used Budmouth Point as a landmark to guide them to Plymouth,' Mr Spratt announced.

Uneasy mutters rippled up and down the street. Cliff and me shared a look: by *landmark* the man meant the lighthouse, didn't he?

'Having made an urgent telephone call to the Ministry of Defence,' he took a dramatic breath, 'I won't mince my words: we must erase the lighthouse.'

There was a pause as the news sank in. I didn't understand what Mr Spratt meant. Wasn't erasing what you did when you'd made a mistake writing in pencil?

The man called Jim, who last time'd been concerned for his cabbages, didn't get it, either: 'Eh? What d'you mean, *erase*?'

'Wipe out, Jim,' Mrs Henderson explained, for she was there too, immaculate in tweeds and pearls but looking agitated. 'Get rid of. Remove.'

I stared at Mr Spratt in astonishment. Would he really destroy Ephraim and Pixie's lovely home? Where would they live? Where would *Cliff and I* live?

Voices started all at once:

'You can't do that!'

'Course they can! You saw those planes!'

'That lighthouse has been there longer than any of us.'

'But if it stops Jerry in his tracks . . .'

Very quickly, my shock turned to confusion. How on earth did you *remove* a lighthouse?

The arguments went round and round. It was like string tying itself in bigger, more complicated knots. Bizarrely, the loudest protests of all came from Mrs Henderson, Miss Carter and Queenie, who'd pushed their way to the front of the crowd.

'I want to know on whose authority you plan to do this,' demanded Miss Carter. Though the coastguard was two steps up, she was tall enough to stare him in the eye.

'It's a perilously dangerous stretch of coast,' Mrs Henderson added. 'There are riptides and quicksands and—'

'It in't so bad. Ships have radio contact nowadays,' a man in fisherman's overalls interrupted.

'Not all of them,' Queenie replied. 'Many smaller boats don't even have motors.'

'Huh, you're an expert now, are you?' the fisherman quipped.

Queenie ignored him. 'Isn't it true that the enemy

won't actually *attack* a lighthouse – all part of the rules of war or something?'

The fisherman laughed drily. 'That's just it, love. There in't no rules any more.'

'We still have our decency, surely,' Mrs Henderson remarked.

'Decency won't keep out the Germans, Mrs H.' The man narrowed his eyes at Queenie. 'Unless you don't *want* to keep them out, that is.'

As mutterings travelled through the crowd, you could sense the mood turning sour. The same had happened earlier outside the school gates, that feeling of distrust. Of people sizing each other up. I didn't like it. Wanting to go, I looked around for a quick way out of the crowd; there wasn't one.

Then Jim the cabbage man said, 'Who in God's name is going to tell Ephraim?'

And everyone started talking again.

'He won't take kindly to it . . .'

'Never known him live anywhere else, not since his family died . . .'

'That was a terrible winter, that was. The churchyard was full to bursting.'

'The lighthouse *is* his family these days . . .'

It made me realise how little I knew of Ephraim.

Though I didn't know how or when his family had died, I understood what it felt like to lose someone. Yet to lose all your family at once must be terrible, and sadness welled up in my throat. He had no one left; we had our mum, and even then it still hurt, knowing Dad would never be back. No wonder poor Ephraim never smiled.

Mr Spratt clapped his hands for quiet. 'I'll be visiting Mr Pengilly directly to inform him of my plans.'

'Good luck – you'll need it,' said Jim, shaking his head.

The crowd dispersed soon after that. Glad to be going home, we walked down the hill, falling back into an even gloomier silence.

Home.

I'd already started thinking of the lighthouse in that way. Poor Ephraim; it'd be a hundred times worse for him and Pixie. Nor could I believe Mr Spratt could just *get rid* of a lighthouse or indeed how he'd do it.

Yet who'd have thought they'd evacuate all the zoo animals out of London or the famous paintings from the National Gallery? And what about us school children, sent from our families to the middle of nowhere? *If* you had a family: from what Queenie'd said, Esther didn't even have that.

All sorts were happening because of this war, not to mention missing sisters and codes I couldn't break. There was so much I still didn't understand. Maybe it *was* possible to remove a lighthouse, though I still wasn't sure how.

WHEN IN DOUBT, LIGHTS OUT

The first thing to disappear was the light itself. Starting that night, Budmouth Point lighthouse, the sea and the quicksands were to remain in absolute darkness. As promised, Mr Spratt came in person with the news but didn't even stay long enough to sit down. Ephraim accepted his duty with a heavy heart, saving his true feelings for when Mr Spratt had left.

'What a stupid idea!' he raged. 'Doesn't he realise how deadly this coast is? We're protecting no one by keeping the light off!'

There were other plans too, which Mr Spratt was 'not yet at liberty to share'. It sounded ominous. Though I tried not to, I imagined awful scenes of people taking down the lighthouse brick by brick.

I didn't like to say I'd only ever seen fishing boats go by. The coastline might be dangerous but it was also very quiet. Whoever used these waters – and someone did because the radio was often busy – was obviously doing so out of sight from us.

*

Cliff went to bed early that night. Knowing I'd not sleep I stayed by the stove trying to read, but my mind kept jumping in and out of the story. That word 'erase' really bothered me: as if you could just wipe out a person's home and move them on somewhere else and expect life to pick up again as normal. Being evacuated had felt like that. You just had to get on with it and try to fit in. The Kindertransport, though, must've been so much worse because on top of everything else Esther had to learn a new language and new customs, which would have made the fitting in part doubly hard.

I shut my book with a sigh. I was trying to understand her, I really was. It wasn't surprising she was angry – *difficult*, Mum would say. I wondered what Esther thought of me: was I annoying? Quiet?

Maybe.

Or was the uncomfortable truth that perhaps, from Esther's viewpoint, it was *me* who was the angry, difficult one?

Mulling it over, I wasn't really listening to Ephraim as he talked on the radio upstairs. But at some point I became aware that his voice was raised.

'They were expected days ago, you know that. It was always going to be tough. With such a small window of time they'd have to be incredibly quick,' he was saying. 'No, I've not had any contact ... no ... not a word.'

I moved to the bottom of the stairs to listen properly.

'The weather was set fair so that shouldn't have been ... She has the co-ordinates ... Yes, I know the whole north coast is German-occupied, that's why they had to act fast. And it'll be dangerous landing a boat here without the light ...'

He went silent. Somewhere in the crackle of the radio I detected a familiar woman's voice – Queenie's. It startled me for a moment, though it also made sense. My hunch from the other night had been right: whatever they were up to, they were in it together.

'Patience, Ephraim,' Queenie said. 'We need to sit this out for a few more days.'

'But it'll only get harder, won't it? Spratt's got other plans for the lighthouse. He told me so this afternoon ...'

'Losing your nerve won't help anyone,' she insisted. 'Look, it sounds like we need a meeting. I'll contact the others. Come over as soon as you can.'

I only just managed to get back into my seat before Ephraim came rushing down the stairs.

'I'm going out for an hour,' he muttered, grabbing his oilskins from their hook.

'Where?' I tried to sound innocent.

'Out,' he repeated. The tension, still there in his voice, made me ever so slightly afraid. Whatever was going on involved a boat, and danger, and someone who'd been expected here but still hadn't arrived.

Once Ephraim had disappeared, I shut my reading book. I *really* couldn't concentrate any more.

*

Straight away the next morning I noticed the breakfast table hadn't been laid. Normally, Ephraim left us porridge on the stove and a jug of fresh milk that came from Mrs Henderson's goats. Today there was no porridge, no milk. The stove hadn't even been lit.

Ephraim wasn't here, either. After what I'd overheard last night, I doubted he'd been home at all: I'd been awake for ages and hadn't heard him come in.

'I'm starving,' Cliff moaned, looking longingly at the stove. 'I could eat a horse.'

I was hungry as well. We weren't meant to touch anything, but we needed food.

'Honestly, I'm going to die of starvation,' Cliff went on. And on, moaning and clutching his stomach. It was starting to grate on me.

'You're not starving in the slightest,' I snapped. 'You don't even know what *starving* is.'

'And you don't care!' Cliff looked visibly hurt.

Feeling mean, I offered him a cup of tea, thinking that might help. But the kettle was cold and I couldn't see a tea caddy anywhere. I grew steadily more frustrated.

'You can't do that!' Cliff cried as I reached for the first cupboard.

I gave him a look. 'Do you want breakfast or not?'

'Course I do.'

Opening the cupboard door, I stepped back in complete surprise. Packet after packet of food tumbled out on to the floor. The shelves had been stuffed full.

'Wow!' I breathed.

'Flaming heck!' cried Cliff.

I'd never seen so much food, not in Queenie's shop or even back home in the Lipton's Tea Room on Edgware Road. There were tins of fruit and peas and peaches. Jar after jar of strawberry jam. Pickled vegetables, biscuits, packets of things that didn't have labels on. Flour in sacks, rice, bags of sugar.

There was so much of everything – easily enough to feed twenty or thirty people, maybe more. Ephraim was expecting someone to arrive, that I knew, but I hadn't realised quite how many 'someones' seemed to be coming.

Once I'd got over the initial shock, I wondered how we'd get all the food back in the cupboard again. The shelves under the sink were equally full: more tins. More rice. A basket of muddy onions. In the next cupboard there were dishes, plates, rolled-up bandages, a few pillows, some blankets.

'Perhaps he got in extra knowing we were coming,' Cliff suggested.

I shook my head. 'Queenie sprang it on him, didn't she? He didn't know we'd be staying so I don't think this stuff is for us.'

In the final cupboard, I found socks – twenty, maybe thirty pairs. There were scarves, hats, a few lumpy-looking sweaters. I couldn't believe Ephraim had knitted all this – and for who? Unlike Mum and Gloria, he obviously wasn't sending any of it away.

Downstairs, the front door slammed. We heard Pixie bark, then footsteps climb the steps.

Ephraim was back.

'Quick! The cupboards!' I cried.

We shut them quickly, quietly, one by one. Then we sat at the table, hearts pounding, just in time to calmly ask Ephraim if he'd got any food in for our breakfast.

*

'I think you're on to something,' I said to Cliff, once we'd eaten and were in our room alone. Pixie was lying between us, nose on paws, grunting contentedly in her sleep. Now seemed a good time to share what I knew. 'It's definitely not for us, that stuff in the cupboards. He's waiting for a whole load of people to turn up.'

'Is he?' Cliff propped himself up on an elbow. 'Who?'

'I don't know yet.'

'He was all nervous at the table just now,' Cliff observed. 'Did you see? He could hardly sit still.'

'He didn't come home last night, either,' I remarked and told Cliff what I'd overheard last night on the radio.

'Wowzers!' Cliff was clearly impressed. 'They're like secret agents, aren't they?'

'No,' I said firmly. 'But what they're working on sounds pretty dangerous. They had a meeting at

Queenie's with some other people too – I'm not sure who.'

It was all so mysterious. Sukie had disappeared; Ephraim was stockpiling food and waiting for a boat to arrive that was already days late, and I couldn't think how that might link to our sister.

I had her note in front of me now, spread across my knee. Having a break from it hadn't helped. It was still completely baffling.

'Every time I look at this code it feels like a stupid dead end,' I moaned.

'Don't look at it, then,' Cliff replied. Getting off the bed he crossed to the window. The binoculars were on the sill where he'd left them. Staring out to sea was fast becoming one of his favourite pastimes.

Narrowing my eyes, I tried the code again. I gave the first line a miss this time and started on the second:

```
I  26  8  T/U  I
```

Then the third.

```
J  26  9  16  19  12  6  8  I
```

All the way through, the highest number was 26.

Which was the number of letters in the alphabet, wasn't it?

I sat up straight. Could that be right? Could each number *be* a letter of the alphabet? Encouraged by the idea, I grabbed a pencil from my school bag and tried working out the second line: so 26 was Z, 8 was H. Though that didn't explain the T or U or I.

I was just about to try the next line down when over by the window Cliff gave a long, low whistle.

'Uh-oh,' he said dramatically. 'Olive, I think they've arrived!'

KEEP IT UNDER YOUR HAT

I rushed to the window, expecting to see a boat spilling strangers out on to the beach. Instead, down on the harbourside a crowd of fifty or more people stared up at the lighthouse. Even without Cliff's binoculars, I could see they were all Budmouth Point locals who, with folded arms and determined faces, were obviously here for a reason.

The lighthouse, I thought grimly. They've come to get rid of it, somehow.

Stepping back from the window, I tidied my hair and smoothed my skirt.

'Right, Cliff, get your coat on,' I said. 'We'd better go and speak to them.'

Cliff frowned. 'Shouldn't we tell Ephraim his visitors are here?'

'I don't think they're the people he's expecting,' I replied.

'All the more reason to let him know.'

'What, and be told to stay inside and touch nothing?' I pointed out, feeling rather bold.

As Cliff put down the binoculars, he looked at me oddly. 'You sounded just like Sukie then.'

*

Descending the ladder with an audience was even more nerve-racking. Cliff had insisted on bringing Pixie along too, and perched on his shoulders she looked the steadiest of any of us. Once we'd reached the cobbles, I relaxed a little.

Then I saw Mr Spratt.

'What's he talking to them about?' Cliff asked, as we made our way towards the crowd.

'Dunno.' Though I was worried it wasn't going to be good news.

When we got within earshot, I heard him say: 'If we use the paint as camouflage, we'll make the whole structure much less apparent to the enemy. It'll be easily done with you all as volunteers – a day or two's paint job at most.'

Paint?

I almost laughed on the spot. So the plan wasn't to *remove* the lighthouse – not literally – but to make it almost invisible with camouflage paint. It was simple. And so obvious. How stupid of me to imagine they'd take the building down. Our home – Ephraim's home – was going nowhere!

There wasn't any time to get used to the idea, either. The painting was to start straight away. Mr Spratt's motor vehicle was so loaded up its back bumper almost touched the cobbles, and when he opened the doors, we saw brushes and paint tins by the crateful inside. More men were arriving now, carrying three very long ladders between them.

It was all happening fast – a bit *too* fast. I didn't think Ephraim would welcome this intrusion, even if it was a better outcome than I'd feared.

Mr Spratt then called out: 'You over there! You're the lighthouse evacuees, aren't you?'

I wasn't overly keen on the coastguard, I decided. Despite his important-looking uniform – or maybe because of it – he seemed to hold himself in high regard. He also had horrid little hands, one of which was pointing at us now. I didn't answer him; he didn't wait for a reply, either.

'Trot along and find Ephraim, there's a good girl.'

I looked at him dumbly. '*Me?*'

'Tell him I'll be with him directly to check his log book entries.'

I was aware of Cliff sidling up to me. 'Why's he interested in Ephraim's log book?' he whispered.

'Because he's the coastguard,' I guessed. 'And Ephraim's meant to write down everything that happens.'

Stuffing my hands into my coat pockets, I didn't move. Or trot. The truth was, I didn't want to be the one to break the news. Ephraim was on edge enough already.

'Well, go on, then! Make yourself useful, girl!' Mr Spratt cried irritably.

I didn't have much choice but to do as he asked.

'Stay here with Pixie,' I muttered to Cliff. 'I won't be long.'

I headed straight for the control room on the top floor.

'Ephraim?' I called up the last flight of stairs. 'Mr Spratt's on his way. Says he wants to see your log book.'

Ephraim didn't reply.

It was unusually quiet – no beep of the radio, no rustling papers or creaking chair. We'd never set foot inside the control room, Cliff and me: we hadn't asked to and Ephraim hadn't invited us. Like everything else at the lighthouse, I assumed it was another thing we weren't meant to touch.

Taking my hat off, I went a little way up the stairs. The harder I listened, the more convinced I was: Ephraim had fallen asleep at his desk.

'Ephraim? Hullo?' I called again.

The silence stretched on. Worried that Mr Spratt would find him, I climbed the remaining stairs, ready to shake Ephraim awake if I had to. On the very last step, I stopped in surprise.

The room was empty. Which, I realised with a sinking feeling, meant Ephraim had gone out again without us knowing.

There was no sign of anything mysterious. In fact the room, with its wooden walls and special equipment, reminded me of our shed at home where we still kept all Dad's tools because no one had the heart to chuck them out. Except everything here was brass, kept gleamingly clean. I wasn't sure what all the dials and levers were used for but they were awfully impressive; the sort of thing Cliff would have swooned over.

Down below a door slammed shut, making me jolt. The faint *ping-ping* of footsteps signalled Mr Spratt's arrival; he was already on the first set of stairs. There was no way of avoiding him. I'd have to cover for Ephraim somehow.

It was then I saw the log book. It lay tantalisingly open on Ephraim's desk not six feet away. Perhaps he'd logged in it where he'd gone, since he was meant to record everything. All the while, the footsteps were getting louder. Mr Spratt had almost reached the floor below.

Seizing my chance, I sidestepped over to the desk. In the log book I saw lists and dates and words to do with the weather. There was only one entry on the right-hand page, dated the day we came to live here.

Journal of Light Station at Budmouth Point
Friday 7th February

Weather: fair. Visibility: good. Sea: calm. Wind: S/
SE veering E. 10 knots.
06.20 hrs: Radio contact Portsmouth.
10.37 hrs: Six German planes sighted.
14.16 hrs: Olive and Cliff Bradshaw arrive.
16.05 hrs: Radio contact St Mary's.
16.57 hrs: Lighting up time.
19.42 hrs: Radio contact Plymouth.

It was the radio entries that struck me: only *three times* in a day? I was certain we'd heard him more often than that – during the evening too, like yesterday with Queenie. But why hadn't he logged it?

Mr Spratt was on the final flight of stairs. I moved back from the table just in time, calling out, 'He's not here, Mr—' before my mouth dropped. 'Oh.'

The head that came into view was dark and tousled: Ephraim.

'Golly!' I gasped in surprise. 'There you are!'

He stopped. 'What're you doing up here?'

'Nothing,' I stuttered. 'Well … um … looking for you, actually. Mr Spratt's coming to check your log book.'

His eyes darted nervously towards the table. 'Is he?' Ephraim came into the room properly now, taking off his oilskin and hanging it over the bannister. He looked exhausted.

'Where've you been?' I asked, before I could stop myself. 'We didn't hear you go out.'

He didn't answer but sank into his chair, brooding over a long white envelope he'd taken from his trouser pocket.

'Ephraim?'

'You'd better go,' he said, not looking up. 'Before Mr Spratt gets here.'

I stayed where I was.

'Whatever it is that you're doing, we could help,' I ventured.

He shook his head wearily. 'You can't help, Olive. It's too complicated. What we're delivering is more dangerous – more important – than customers' groceries.'

I looked at him. 'So you are delivering *something*, then?'

'I can't tell you that,' he said. 'Now, really, you need to—'

'Queenie trusted us to help,' I tried again. 'Because she knew Sukie, my sister, before she … well … what with them being penpals and everything.'

Ephraim's eyebrows shot up. '*Penpals?* Where did you get that idea?'

I didn't understand.

'Sukie used to write to Queenie up in her room at home – really long letters, almost every night …' I stopped.

A quizzical look had crossed his face, making me wonder if I'd been on to something there as well. It was hard to imagine Sukie and Queenie as friends; given Queenie's frosty welcome, it made much more sense if they weren't.

For a long moment Ephraim stared at his feet.

Eventually he glanced up. 'Can I trust you?'

I nodded eagerly. Probably a bit *too* eagerly.

'It wasn't—' He looked past me to the top of the stairs, where Mr Spratt now stood. Neither of us had heard him coming. Ephraim sprang to his feet, startled. I stepped back clumsily.

'Mr Spratt, sir!' Ephraim coughed, offering a handshake. He tucked his other hand behind his back; in it still was the long white envelope.

I was aware of Mr Spratt moving closer to the table. Of the silver buttons on his coat and the salty, oily smell of him. But I couldn't take my eyes off Ephraim's envelope. It was moving. Wagging. Like he was trying to get my attention with it.

'Morning, young man,' Mr Spratt began, striding over to the nearest window like he owned the place. 'You'll have noticed my team of painters outside ready to start work on the camouflaging. The sooner we commence ...' He droned on but I was too distracted to listen.

'What d'you want me to do?' I whispered to Ephraim.

'Take it to Queenie,' he replied, stuffing the envelope into my hand. 'And so you know: she wasn't your sister's penpal.'

I stared at him. 'What d'you mean?'

'I was. Sukie was writing to me.'

Turning the Tide

Hurrying through the harbour, I had to dodge more people, paint pots, ladders than I could count. I'd left Cliff on the beach playing with Pixie; after what Ephraim had just told me I needed a moment to myself.

Could *he* have been the man Sukie met that night?

Ephraim ... and ... my *sister*?

I pictured the letters inside those chocolate boxes in Sukie's drawer. Maybe there *was* something romantic between them, despite what Mrs Henderson said about Ephraim wanting to be alone.

Yet in my mind, the code looked practical. To the point. Besides, the man I'd seen Sukie with was tall and blond and smartly dressed: Ephraim was none of these things.

He'd been writing to my sister, though. And she'd written back – long, detailed letters that'd kept her busy in her room most nights. I wondered what they'd talked about, what they had in common. But, I was beginning to realise, there was plenty about my sister I didn't understand.

Head down against the wind, I walked faster. Now that Ephraim had trusted me with his message to Queenie, perhaps I should trust him too. He'd been in contact with Sukie, hadn't he, so he *must* know something.

I made my mind up: it was time to share the code with someone who might be able to break it. I'd ask Ephraim as soon as I got back.

*

The post office was busy. What I'd not considered was the prospect of running into Esther, who was serving behind the counter. I bet she'd not forgotten the ink-can incident, even if I momentarily had.

Joining the queue, I fidgeted nervously. Esther, I could see, was wearing the same brown apron Cliff had worn, only it actually fitted her. She served the woman in front with a politeness I didn't expect, which made me hope she might at least be civil to me.

'There's your coupons back, Mrs Saunders,' she said, sliding a ration book across the counter. 'Sorry about that. We'll let you know when more biscuits come in.'

'Never known it happen before,' the woman complained, glaring at me as if it was my fault all the biscuits had been sold.

Seeing I was next, Esther's expression changed. 'I'm not speaking to you,' she said, staring over my head.

My heart gave a disappointed thump.

'I've not come to make trouble. I'm here for Queenie.' I glanced behind her at the door that connected to the rest of the house. I'd wanted to say something else – something kinder – but felt suddenly, stupidly tongue-tied.

Esther folded her arms like she wasn't going to move out of my way. Underneath the hard stare, she looked tired. This was the bluster Queenie had mentioned, wasn't it, the tough act under which was another, nicer girl. I just needed to give her a chance. The trouble was, every time I tried, it seemed to go wrong.

The shop bell jangled as another customer came in. Esther, moving back behind the counter, finally jerked her head towards the door.

'You know where Queenie is,' she muttered. 'Same place as always.'

*

The cellar door was ajar. I knocked, but hearing no reply, straightened my shoulders and went down the steps.

'Olive!' Queenie blinked. Whatever she'd been doing, she'd stopped it abruptly. You could almost sense the room holding its breath.

It was strange to think that just above our heads the post office customers were being served as normal. Yet down here felt a different world – shadowy, secretive – and I had a thrilling sense that I'd crossed over into it.

I gave Queenie the envelope. 'This is from Ephraim.'

Eyebrows raised in surprise, she looked at me, then the letter, then me again.

I was good at delivering – quick, reliable – and Queenie knew it. I wanted her to know that Ephraim trusted me too. 'He said to bring it straight away.'

She didn't bother with a letter opener, ripping the seal with her fingernails. I wondered if I was supposed to wait for a reply.

The cellar was messier than last time I'd been here. It felt busier too, as if all sorts of urgent things had been going on, and the buzz still hung in the air. Documents – on headed notepaper – lay spread across the table. Others, marked with crosses, spilled out of a box on the floor. None of it looked like post office business to me: the table was heaped with weather charts and lists of tide times as if she was planning a boat trip.

Queenie took her time reading Ephraim's note. My hands fidgeted in my coat pockets as I waited. I couldn't stop looking around me, either. If Queenie noticed, she made no attempt today to block my view.

A tray of dirty tea things sat forgotten about on the floor. There were more chairs than normal, all evidence of yesterday's meeting. One teacup, I noticed, had lipstick on its rim, the same glossy red colour that Miss Carter wore. Ephraim had mentioned 'the others': it didn't take much guessing to work out who they were. When it came to welcoming strangers to Budmouth Point, Miss Carter and Mrs Henderson had experience.

First evacuees, now refugees. That was it, wasn't it?

There were people in Europe, fleeing for their lives, who were escaping here, to Budmouth Point. *These* were the visitors Ephraim was expecting. The realisation made me dizzy.

It connected to Sukie didn't it, because she'd cried trying to tell me how 'heartbreaking' it was not being able to help – yet in writing to Ephraim, maybe she'd found a way to. Perhaps their letters were actually full of plans of how they might get people away from the

Nazis. It would certainly explain why Sukie wrote so much and so often. Bit by bit I could feel it coming together in my head.

That map with the foreign place names I'd found in her drawer at home – was this where the boat was coming from?

'Are you all right?' Queenie asked suddenly. Looking concerned, she offered me a chair.

'I'm fine.' I stayed standing.

'No you're not.' Queenie pinched the bridge of her nose like she had a headache. 'You're a smart girl, Olive. I'd a feeling you'd guess what was going on. I didn't think Ephraim could keep it from you for long.'

'He told me about writing to Sukie, that's all,' I said, though it wasn't strictly true. But I was unsure how much to say.

'You're learning that some things need to be secret.' Queenie gave me a wry smile. 'I trust you can keep this one?'

I hesitated. She hadn't actually told me what the secret was, but I'd already pretty much guessed. 'You're expecting some people, from a place that's occupied by the Germans?'

'Yes . . . from France.' She sat back in her chair, raking her fingers through her hair. 'We're bringing them here for a few days, giving them false papers, then helping them on their way again.'

'Where will they go?'

'To countries that aren't as strict as ours about Jewish refugees: America, Canada, Australia maybe.'

I thought for a moment. 'Is what you're doing against the law?'

'Probably. If we keep a low profile, we might just get away with it.' She sighed heavily. 'They've got to get here first, though. It's such a risky mission. They were smuggled out of Austria all the way to the French coast, and quite frankly they've been lucky to make it that far. We were expecting the boat ten days ago ...'

I nodded, my mind whizzing: *Day 9*. The only part of Sukie's note I understood.

'Do you know why Ephraim and my sister wrote to each other?' I asked suddenly.

'What? Oh, Gloria mentioned Sukie was looking for a penpal – it was a new "thing" apparently.' She rolled her eyes rather dismissively. 'Ephraim was so lonely, we both thought it might cheer him up. It certainly worked – he's quite taken with your Sukie.'

'There's more to it than that,' I ventured. 'My sister's involved in this mission, isn't she?'

Queenie frowned. 'Your sister? Why would she be?'

'You don't know what she's like,' I replied, for it was very clear now that Queenie'd never written to Sukie, nor probably ever met her. If she had she'd realise how much my sister hated the Nazis, how upset the news coming out of Europe made her, how headstrong and brave she was.

Doing something to try and help people threatened by Hitler was *exactly* the sort of thing my sister would want to be part of. I couldn't understand why Queenie was so certain she wasn't.

*

By now it was late morning. Back at the harbour I was shocked to see just how much of the lighthouse had already been painted out. High up on ladders little figures were working so quickly that almost half of the tower was now covered in greyish-brown paint. Without its red and white stripes the lighthouse looked unrecognisable – which was the plan, I knew, but it still brought a lump to my throat. It wasn't fair, this stupid war of ours. Why did everything decent and good have to suffer?

It was then I noticed how far down the beach Cliff had gone, his blue coat just a speck in the distance.

He was too close to the quicksand sign for my liking. As for Pixie, I couldn't see her at all.

Scrambling down on to the shingle, I set off to fetch them both, which was easier said than done. The incoming tide had turned the beach into a narrow, steep strip so I kept sliding towards the sea then having to climb back up again, and I was soon hot and out of breath.

Two hundred yards or so up ahead was the quicksand sign. I still couldn't see Pixie, only Cliff staring over that wooden fence-type thing called a groyne. Something was wrong. I started running.

'What are you doing down here?' I yelled, reaching Cliff. 'Where's Pixie?'

In answer, a dog barked. It sounded whiny and frightened. The dread I'd been fighting flooded me.

'You idiot!' I cried. 'Can't you read the sign? It says "Quicksand"!'

'It wasn't my fault!' Cliff sobbed. 'Pixie took off after a seagull. I tried to call her back.'

I breathed deeply. Counted to ten. 'Just tell me where the dog is.'

Cliff pointed to the groyne. Thankfully, a few feet beyond was a white-and-brown dog – at least the head, shoulders and tail of one. The tide was coming in so fast she'd be underwater in minutes.

'Stand back,' I ordered Cliff. '*Right* back. On the safe side of the groyne.'

I'd no idea what to do next but sounding like I did seemed to do the trick. Cliff moved back on to the shingle. Rolling up my coat sleeves, I climbed up on the groyne. Beyond it the sand was wet and rippled by the tide. I didn't trust myself to step on to it. I'd have to try and reach Pixie from here. Gripping the wood, I stretched my free arm towards the dog.

'Keep still, girl,' I called. 'Nearly there.'

Except I wasn't.

Only three measly feet of sand stood between us, but it might as well have been the Sahara. I couldn't reach her. The sand had covered her shoulders and was creeping up her neck. She'd started whining so miserably I couldn't bear it.

I swung my legs over the groyne.

Cliff cried out: 'What're you doing? You can't – !'

'I'm just going to try a couple of steps,' I told him. I'd read enough adventure stories to know it wasn't that simple with quicksand. But I didn't want Cliff to panic.

One step in, the sand was sticky. Another step and it thickened like soup. At the third, I couldn't see my feet any more. The sand was closing in around my ankles, my calves, all cold and clammy like porridge. Worse was how it tugged at my shoes. The harder you resisted it, the stronger it pulled. It was a horrible feeling, and made me want to kick and shout and run to safety.

Luckily, I didn't need to go further in. From there I slipped my fingers through Pixie's collar.

'Good girl.' I tried to sound normal. 'Are you ready? On the count of three. One . . . two . . .'

As I went to step backwards, my feet didn't move. Instead, my whole body lurched at the waist. Pixie gave a feeble little whine. I smoothed her head, telling her to hush. Then it was me crying 'Ouch!' as something lashed against my leg.

'Wrap it round your waist!' Cliff shouted.

It was a decent length of rope, and I was so grateful for it I could've sobbed. Not that I believed for a moment Cliff'd be able to pull me out, but it had to be worth a try.

With the rope tied around me, I got a firmer hold on Pixie. On the count of three, my little brother began to heave. I could hear him behind me, grunting, puffing as he stepped up the beach.

'That's it!' I yelled in encouragement. 'Keep going!'

At first all that happened was the rope pulled tight around my waist. The pressure grew. And grew, till it felt like I'd be sliced through the kidneys. Just as I thought I'd be cut in half, the rope went slack.

'I need to catch my breath,' Cliff panted.

Glancing at the tide, I didn't think there was time. 'Let's try again, please, Cliff!'

Once more, the rope went tight. Really tight. It dug into my ribs, burning the skin under my clothes.

'Go on! Keep going! Pull! PULL!' I screamed.

'I'm trying!' Cliff yelled back.

I realised Pixie's shoulders had worked free of the sand.

'PULL!' I cried, almost hysterical. 'KEEP PULLING!'

It was hard to hold on to Pixie, who with a little bit of freedom was now struggling against me. I could feel my hands slipping from her collar. My legs seemed to lift beneath me. There was one enormous slurp. A huge gasp, and I fell back on to the shingle with Pixie in my arms.

Breathless, Cliff flopped down beside me. 'Are you all right?'

'Think so,' though my arms and legs felt weak and rubbery. 'You were terrific – the cat's bananas!'

He grinned. '*Pyjamas*, dummy!'

I didn't want to think what would've happened without Cliff or the rope. As I untied the knot at my waist though, I noticed how the rest of the rope ran on up to the top of the beach as if it was tied to something else.

I beckoned to Cliff, who was trying to get the worst of the sand off Pixie. 'Have you seen this?'

He hadn't.

Intrigued, we followed it as it disappeared into a clump of seaweed, then reappeared a few yards on, twisting around a breakwater post. It went over driftwood, under pebbles, leading us to what looked like a large box covered in sand.

'Careful, Olive!' Cliff cried. 'It might be a German mine!'

But kneeling down, I realised it had a handle – a leather one – and there were clips and buckles gone rusty from the seawater.

'It's not a mine, you great goose,' I said. 'It's a suitcase,' which, judging by the foreign words on its soggy label, had come all the way from Europe.

HITLER WILL SEND NO WARNING

The suitcase wasn't going any further. Waterlogged, it weighed a ton, and when we tried to move it even a few feet along the beach, we had to give up, panting. I knew Ephraim would want to see it, but there was no way on earth we'd get it up the lighthouse ladder.

'I'm going to open it,' I decided. Crouching beside it on the shingle, I flicked the catches. Cliff shuffled closer, breathing fast.

It'd probably once been an expensive piece of luggage. Now the sea had warped it and the leather was all scratched. With a gritty creak, the lid lifted. Inside were blouses, a few dresses – damp ones – with sandy, salty stuff caught in the folds. Tucked down the side were a couple of books. I couldn't understand their titles; the words were in a different language. There was a pot of face cream, a toothbrush with its bristles splayed a little. I wondered who'd used it last – and where.

'Is there a name on it?' Cliff asked.

I pointed to the inside of the suitcase lid. There was a sticker that might once have said 'Vienna', which I knew was in Austria. In tiny writing underneath was an address I couldn't read because the ink had all but washed away.

This suitcase belonged to someone. And that *someone* had packed up their books and clothes and toothbrush, much like we had, and had left their home far behind. I wondered if they'd felt frightened, unsure of where they were going and what sort of welcome they'd receive when they got there. At least we'd arrived in one piece.

The more I looked, the more I was sure this luggage was from Queenie's missing boat. I could feel it too, a sort of foreboding in the air, because if my instinct was right, then where were the passengers? Had their attempt to help people gone tragically wrong? And what about Sukie? The awfulness of what this washed-up suitcase implied almost overwhelmed me.

'Olive?' Cliff tugged on my sleeve. 'You're crying.'

'Am I?' Quickly, I wiped my face on my sleeve. 'Come on. Let's go and tell Ephraim.'

We left the suitcase where it was.

*

Back at the lighthouse, there was a note on the table.

Gone to Tythe Cove. Make lunch if I'm not back, E.

Tythe Cove was the next village along the coast. You reached it by a path that went up steeply over the clifftops. I'd never walked it but could well imagine why Ephraim might want to: the views down on to the beach made it an excellent lookout for anything that might've washed ashore. And you'd not need to record your observations in a log book or mention it in conversation on the lighthouse radio. I only hoped he found something more cheering than a suitcase.

By the time we'd cleaned up and changed out of our sandy clothes, it was lunchtime and Ephraim hadn't returned. I rather enjoyed rummaging freely in the kitchen cupboards and, finding parsnips and a bottle of banana flavouring, I made Cliff's favourite mock-banana sandwiches. It was a total shock when he said he wasn't very hungry.

'Are you feeling all right?' I asked.

'My belly button hurts.'

'You probably hurt yourself pulling me out of that quicksand,' I told him. 'A torn muscle or something.'

'Have a look, will you?' He pulled up his sweater, but I couldn't see anything wrong with his belly button, apart from it being full of grit and fluffy grey stuff.

'You need another wash,' I said.

Yet by the time we put our coats on ready for school, he'd come out in a cold sweat so I insisted he go to bed.

*

As usual, the Budmouth Point kids were gathered at the school gates – not as many as there'd been that first day, but enough to remind me we were still a bit of a novelty. Today though, something else had their attention.

'Listen to that engine. He's in trouble,' said a red-haired boy.

I heard the spluttering of what I thought was a broken-down van, until I realised they were looking at the sky. Moments later, the plane came fully into view. The black cross of the Luftwaffe, visible on its tail, made my stomach drop. So much for the camouflage paint protecting us: just like the others before him, this pilot was turning right, away from the open sea towards land, using the lighthouse to guide him.

It was obvious something was wrong with the plane.

Thick black smoke trailed from the engine on the left. Flames were visible under the wing. There was another spluttering. Then silence. Another splutter. Silence. It was horrible yet compelling to watch.

About four hundred yards off the coast, the plane started losing height. It didn't drop down gently, either. There was a terrific lurch. The whole aircraft shuddered. It veered left, then right, almost drunkenly. I was afraid it was going to keep going and crash into the village. The truth was worse: it wouldn't make it that far.

Two hundred yards out to sea, the plane dropped further. The left wing dipped down. Straightened. The right one did the same. The horror of what was happening flashed before me: the German plane was on a collision course with the lighthouse. It'd never clear the top of the building. But it had to. Cliff and Pixie were still inside. Not that I could do anything, it was too late for that. I couldn't even scream: my heart was jammed in my throat.

'He's aiming right for it!' one of the Budmouth kids cried out.

'Flipping heck! He's going to hit it!'

'He must have a parachute. Why doesn't he bail out?'

I couldn't watch. Yet I couldn't bear not to. *Shut*

up, I willed them all, hand pressed to my mouth, *just shut up*.

Everything slowed. The plane spluttered again, then seemed to bounce on the air. It came at the lighthouse almost level with the front door. I braced myself for the impact. The engine gave a dying roar. At the very last moment, it swerved right. Miraculously, it missed.

It took a moment for my brain to catch up. The plane was on its side, its left wing clipping the waves. With a final lurch, it dipped behind the rooftops and trees, disappearing from sight. Seconds later we heard a huge *DOOF* as it hit the ground. Fresh smoke billowed into the sky.

All at once everyone was trying to work out where the plane had come down.

'It's over by the Wilcoxes' farm.'

'No, it's by the harbour, just past Jim's house.'

'I reckon it's hit the woods.'

Still stunned, I didn't much care where it was. Cliff being safe was what mattered to me.

At the school gates people from my class started appearing, Mr Barrowman amongst them. School, it seemed, had been forgotten.

'Where's everyone going?' I asked a boy called Luke Mitchell.

'To see the plane, of course.' He grinned. 'And what's left of the pilot.'

It sounded a bit horrid, to be honest. Though I was intrigued to see what a German actually looked like, and I knew Cliff would want to hear the gory details. So I went with them.

*

Just beyond the harbour was a blackened hedge: the pilot had ploughed right through it, coming to a halt in the field beyond. The plane's nose was buried in the ground, the tail sticking into the air. Pretty much everyone in Budmouth Point had come along for a look. The mood was wary, hushed, as if the plane was a sleeping dog that might suddenly wake up and bite. I should've been amazed at the sight of it, but instead it made me feel a bit uncomfortable to be gawping at someone else's misfortune.

Just shy of the wreckage, the crowd stopped. Quickly word spread that the pilot wasn't dead. He was sitting in the grass with a broken arm and you could see the bone sticking out through his shirtsleeve.

'Do we tend him or leave him?' asked Mrs Moore.

'I don't fancy touching him.' This was Mrs Drummond.

'Call the police,' someone else suggested.

'Or the coastguard.'

There was a lot of confusion, with no one really knowing what to do.

Then a familiar voice said: 'I want to see his arm.'

I was aware of Mr Barrowman pushing past as he tried to grab someone's coat collar. 'Don't stick your nose in, Miss Jenkins. Stay back here out of the way.' But Esther was quicker than him, her dark pigtailed head soon lost in the crowd.

Everyone started shuffling forwards, moving closer to the aircraft as a group, as if there was safety in numbers. I shuffled with them, though the idea of seeing sticking-out bones was beginning to lose its appeal.

We came to a stop just in front of the aircraft. The smell of engine fuel was strong enough to make your eyes water. I could see the ground all churned up and the plane's cockpit smashed on one side. It was incredible to think anyone had even survived.

Yet there he was, head bowed, kneeling on the grass maybe twenty feet away. The pilot's uniform was in tatters. The damaged arm hung limp at his side. I didn't see a bone, thankfully, but it was certainly bleeding badly. He was skinny in a way that made him look young – perhaps not much older than Ephraim. I'd not expected that; I'd not expected him to be crying, either. It made me more uncomfortable than ever.

The crowd now had the pilot surrounded.

'Put your hands on your head where we can see them!' This was Mrs Wilcox, the farmer's wife, who looked scarier than any German.

But the pilot couldn't lift his wounded arm. And he could barely stand, swaying dizzily and gasping in pain. He soon sank to his knees again.

'He's putting it on, don't trust him,' said a woman I didn't know.

From the back of the crowd, someone shouted: 'Spratt's here. Let him through!'

A pathway opened up and the coastguard appeared, stern-faced and broad-chested.

'Everybody calm down,' he insisted, patting the air with his little hands. 'We'll deal with this situation. Go home now, please.'

No one moved. Just yesterday the locals had welcomed him like a hero: today's mood was different. People folded their arms, shook their heads. It was, I had to admit, rather satisfying to see bewilderment on the coastguard's face.

'Painting the lighthouse didn't work, did it, Mr Spratt?' a woman in overalls called out. 'The Germans still found it easy enough.'

'Waste of bloomin' time,' old Mr Watkins agreed.

'The painting isn't yet finished.' Mr Spratt quickly regained his composure. 'Rest assured we'll have the job completed by sundown today.'

My heart sank. This wasn't going to help the missing boat one bit. What if it was still on its way from France? What if they were trying to find a lighthouse that didn't appear to be there?

Mr Spratt's answer didn't quieten the crowd, either. If anything everyone moved closer to the pilot. Before I knew it I was just a few feet away. Mrs Wilcox and another woman were standing over him in a threatening manner. The pilot sensed it too, covering his head protectively with his good arm.

'That's for what you're doing to our boys.' Mrs Wilcox spat at him. The other woman prodded him with her foot. The pilot pleaded, using words I didn't know. But he was sobbing – that I *did* understand.

'Don't!' I burst out. 'He's injured!'

Someone told me to be quiet.

Surprisingly, Mr Barrowman stuck up for me: 'Olive's right. We should do things properly and follow international law. Hand him over—'

'Oh belt up, Barrowman!' snapped the fisherman who'd argued with Queenie yesterday. 'The chap's a German. When've they ever done anything *properly*, eh?'

Shouts of 'Call the police!' and 'Give Jerry what for!' rippled through the crowd. Yet still no one knew what to do. It infuriated me how Mr Spratt did nothing. He'd been so particular with Ephraim about the lighthouse, checking and double-checking the log book, yet now he very conveniently chose to look the other way.

I only hoped that when Dad's plane came down someone kind had found him, to hold his hand when he was hurting and tell him not to be scared. Better still if it'd been so quick he'd died before his plane hit the ground.

No, I wouldn't keep quiet. I had a voice, and it was time to make some noise with it.

X MARKS THE SPOT

'German or not, the pilot's a human being!' I shouted over the general hubbub. 'So are we – we're not animals!'

Mrs Wilcox glared at me, unimpressed. 'Who are you calling an animal, young lady?'

'What I'm saying,' I insisted, 'is that we should treat him the same way we'd hope they'd treat a pilot of ours.'

'There's a war on, you stupid girl,' the fisherman chipped in. 'An enemy's an enemy.'

'Come here, Olive. Let the adults sort it out.' Mrs Drummond tried to take my arm, but I shurgged her off.

'Imagine if it was your son or brother, or ... your father,' I pleaded. 'You'd want things done properly, wouldn't you?'

For a few people that seemed to hit home. There were nods and sounds of approval. Then a hand grabbed me by the scruff of the neck, startling me.

Mrs Wilcox pushed me towards the pilot.

'Go on, then,' she snarled, releasing me with such force I stumbled to my knees. 'You sort it out.'

The German was so close I caught a whiff of something bloody, sickly, like a butcher's-shop smell. I could see his injured arm properly now, except it didn't look quite real. It was bluish-white bone, skin gaping and red like the inside of someone's mouth.

The ground tilted beneath my feet, and the next thing I knew someone had pushed my head between my knees.

Mrs Henderson was beside me, her arm round my shoulders. 'You had a little faint, lovey.'

And then a voice much louder than mine cut through the noise: 'What *on earth* is going on?'

Everyone fell quiet. Looking up, I saw Queenie, hands on hips, her gaze flitting over the crowd. I felt rather silly for fainting.

She spotted Mr Spratt. 'Did you allow this to happen?' she asked in amazement.

'Now just a minute,' Mr Spratt protested. 'I suggest you watch your tone—'

Queenie talked over his head: 'You should be ashamed of yourselves, all of you.'

People stared at their feet, embarrassed. As Queenie made towards the pilot, Mrs Wilcox stood in her way.

'Can I remind you that this is my land?'

'And this is my country, Mrs Wilcox, during a time of war. So I'd advise you to step aside and let me escort the prisoner to where the military police can arrest him.'

Mrs Wilcox didn't reply. I gulped uneasily, wondering if the mood of the crowd was about to change again.

'If you don't move out of my way,' Queenie said frostily, 'you'll be in breach of international law, and with this crowd as my witness, I'll be taking *you* to the military police, as well as our enemy here.'

The two women squared up to each other. Finally, with a terse sigh, Mrs Wilcox moved back. The rest of the crowd parted to let Mrs Henderson and Miss Carter through. They went straight to help Queenie, who was trying to get the pilot to sit up, but even the tiniest movement made him yelp in pain.

'This arm needs a splint,' Mrs Henderson was saying.

The ground swung a bit as I stood up, but as long as I didn't look at the pilot I was fine.

'The doctor needs fetching, Olive. Can you manage that?' Mrs Henderson asked. 'He's called Dr Morrison and he lives in the last house before the church.'

I nodded: I knew where it was.

'Good girl. Quick as you can.'

Glancing over her shoulder, I noticed Queenie crouched beside the pilot holding his hand. She was speaking to him very quietly. The one word I caught was 'Nine'.

In a sudden moment of panic, I was sure she was talking about Sukie's note. But then I twigged the tone of her voice: calm, clear, sensible.

Sukie once said we should learn a few German words just in case they invaded us. She'd taught us 'no' and 'yes', 'please don't shoot' and 'do you have oranges?' So I knew 'nine' wasn't just an English word. It was a German one too, spelled '*Nein*'.

*

True to Mr Spratt's word, by sunset that day the paint job was finished. Budmouth Point lighthouse now looked like an enormous sandcastle, and was probably about as much use as one. Surrounded on all sides by grey sea, grey sky and an even greyer beach, it was devilishly hard to pick it out.

It made me ever more concerned for the missing boat from France. There were quicksands, rocks, all manner of hazards – Ephraim had told us. How awful it would be to escape the Nazis only to die the moment you hit the Devon coast.

As soon as I told Ephraim about the washed-up suitcase, he went off in search of it. Meanwhile Cliff said he still felt 'iffy' so Pixie belly-crawled under the blankets to keep him company, and I sat at the foot of his bed.

'I saw the German pilot through the binoculars – he was trying to turn the plane so he didn't hit us.' Cliff looked flushed in the cheeks. I wasn't sure if it was the excitement of the near miss or a nasty fever causing it.

'Queenie spoke to him in German,' I told him. 'What d'you make of that?'

Cliff pulled a face. 'That she's clever?'

It wasn't as exciting an idea as her being a double agent or spying for Great Britain, but it was probably nearer the truth. I was beginning to be rather in awe of Queenie. She had that quiet authority that made you respect her, even if she wasn't overly friendly. Unlike Sukie, she didn't need everyone to like her. In her old, baggy sweaters I don't think she even cared. She simply did what she thought was right, and stuck to her guns. It was this, to me, that made her impressive.

'Queenie's convinced Sukie's not involved in any of this,' I mused. 'What d'you think?'

But Cliff had already fallen asleep.

*

For a while I sat listening to the wind as it got stronger, making eerie whistling sounds at the windows. Then I started imagining huge waves crashing over a tiny boat, and whoever's suitcase we'd found clinging on for dear life. Hoping to distract myself I wrote a quick postcard to Mum.

Tuesday 18th February 1941

Dear Mum,

We went for a walk on the beach today with Ephraim's dog Pixie. She was so well behaved. You won't believe how much she loves Cliff, though this might be because he's always eating.

All splendid here. Like a holiday!

So long, Olive x

Mrs Rachel Bradshaw

16 Fairfoot Road

Bow

London

England

It was all lies, of course. Stupid, silly lies to stop Mum being sadder than she already was. Writing it didn't slow my churning brain, either. So when Ephraim returned with the suitcase and called me to the sitting room, I took Sukie's note with me.

*

The suitcase from Vienna sat dripping on the floor. With the oil lamps lit, the stove hot and the blackouts closed, it should've felt cosy. Yet from somewhere a chilly draught breathed around our necks.

'The suitcase probably is from the French boat,' Ephraim admitted miserably.

'Or it could mean they're very close,' I suggested. 'Maybe they've landed already?'

Ephraim shook his head. 'It looks like it's been in the water for a few days.'

Which made me more afraid than ever to ask about Sukie but I had to know whether Ephraim, like Queenie, thought she wasn't involved.

'When you wrote to my sister, what did she talk to you about?' I asked tentatively.

'Sukie?' Ephraim rubbed the back of his neck, embarrassed. 'That's not really any of your business, Olive.'

'Not the slushy stuff,' I said quickly, feeling myself go red. 'I meant anything about helping people trying to escape Hitler.'

'Actually, she hasn't written to me for a couple of weeks. I don't know what I've said to upset her.'

I blinked; caught my breath. 'You don't know she's gone missing?'

'No!' He was visibly shocked. It surprised me; since discovering their connection I'd assumed he knew – that he was part of it, even. 'What happened? Tell me!'

So I told him about the night at the cinema. About the tall man she'd gone off to meet and how I'd followed her, until she noticed and got angry with me. I showed him the note. It was a sorry sight – smoke-smeared and water-stained, and still smelling of air raids.

Ephraim leaned forwards to take it from me, but I didn't let go.

'Queenie says Sukie's not working with you,' I said. 'But I'm pretty sure she is.'

Ephraim shook his head. 'She isn't, Olive. Our contact in London was a Mrs Arby. She was nothing to do with Sukie.'

The name didn't mean anything to me, either. I slumped back in my seat.

'We chose Mrs Arby – we all chose her – because she was one of the best,' Ephraim added. 'It was such a difficult run, sailing overnight from the northernmost tip of France to here. And now without the lighthouse functioning and this dreadful weather . . .' He stopped dismally, but I was keen to keep him talking.

'Tell me about the code. How does it work?'

Ephraim glanced at the note in my hand. I still didn't give it him, and I think he saw my determination: I wanted to crack the code myself.

'Everything's an opposite,' he said. 'Try it.'

Spreading the note over my knee, I studied it once again.

```
DAY 9
I  26 8  T/U I
J  26 9  16 19 12 6 8 I
B  26 T  - 50.26
B  12 13 20 + 3.6
```

If the code worked on opposites then *day* would be *night*. And on a clock face the direct opposite of *9* was *3*. Which must mean Day 9 was *night* at *three*. Three o'clock in the morning, the sort of time people did things they didn't want anyone else to know about.

Opposites, I reminded myself: Day = night, so the opposite of the alphabet might be ... numbers? Could A = 1, B = 2, right up to Z = 26? I tried it on the next line of the note, I 26 8 T/U I, swapping letters for numbers, and numbers for letters ... until I ended up with a different code: 9 Z H 20/21 9. It still didn't mean anything.

What if the numbers/letters idea worked as opposites, from A = 26 down to Z = 1? Each line started and ended with a letter. Were they opposites *too*? I tried swapping A with Z and so on, but that didn't work either. I was stuck again. I went back to the opposites idea: day/night, light/dark – yet it still didn't seem to fit.

I'd always been rubbish at codes. Last summer holidays, Cliff and his friends invented one you had to read backwards in the mirror, and I couldn't even break that. Though you'd hardly expect an important wartime message to be written in a simple schoolboy code.

Or would you?

I looked at the note again. Could the alphabet be a sort of reflection? If you halved it and went backwards ... so A became M ... Which meant the first line read as E 26 8 T/S E.

Now for the numbers. For my brain this bit was harder. Keep thinking backwards, I told myself. So I swapped all the numbers for letters, starting from the opposite end of the alphabet with 26 = A. The result this time was different:

```
Day 9
East/SE
Darkhouse
Lat -50.26
Long +3.6
```

I was getting somewhere. The message almost made sense, especially if you remembered that 'East/SE' was really 'West/SW'. The last lines, looking like directions on a map, were also probably opposites. And it was obvious what 'Darkhouse' meant.

I wasn't sure any of this was good news, though.

'Well?' Ephraim asked expectantly.

I shook my head. Cracking the code had confirmed my worst fears. 'She was coming here. The note says "Darkhouse" and there are numbers like you get on maps. She was on the missing boat.'

Ephraim frowned: 'That can't be right.'

'It must be. That man she met gave her the details and she hid them in her pocket, but then she lost the coat, didn't she? So your boat full of visitors tried to make the crossing without the information. That's why their journey went wrong.'

Ephraim blew out his cheeks.

'Well?' I asked. 'That's it, isn't it?'

'No, it isn't.'

'But I did the opposites thing you said and—'

'Show me the note again,' Ephraim demanded.

This time I handed him the piece of paper. He read it in seconds.

'What d'you think it says?' I asked.

Ephraim scratched his head so his hair stood up on end. 'The boat was meant to come here, you're right. But I still can't see how Sukie would've got hold of this information.'

'What do we do now?'

Ephraim stood up.

'I need to speak to the others,' he said, clearly agitated. 'This changes everything. If the instructions never got to Mrs Arby in the first place, those poor people might still be in France. I dread to think what's happened to them if that's the case.'

'So d'you believe me now? You think Sukie's involved?'

He hesitated. 'I really hope not.'

It was a grim answer. For it meant the boat I was certain my sister was on was unlikely ever to arrive.

TOGETHER

Ephraim disappeared down the ladder, the wind making his oilskins flap like a ship's sails. I was tempted to give him a head start, then follow anyway – and he guessed as much.

'You stay here,' he instructed me. 'I'll be back with any news as soon as I can.'

I shut the front door miserably. Waiting was going to be torture: I was already imagining the worst and the best in one chaotic thought. It didn't help that the lighthouse had started swaying slightly, which Ephraim said happened when the wind was particularly strong.

Clutching the handrail, I climbed the stairs to check on Cliff. Part of me was bursting to tell him that I'd cracked the code, but the rest of what we'd worked out wasn't exactly joyful, so I didn't think it fair to worry him. He was asleep, anyway, the blankets kicked off, the sheets twisted around his legs. I tucked him in again, then went back up to the sitting room to wait.

An hour passed and Ephraim didn't return. The storm had gathered strength, hurling sleet against the windows with such force I thought they'd break. It was a bit like being inside my own head, everything noisy and rattling about.

It got harder to keep the stove alight as the wind blustered down the chimney, and I had to wrap myself in a blanket to stay warm. For supper I made a cheese sandwich, which I shared with Pixie.

Another hour passed. Then another.

I walked circuits of the room, looking out of each window in the hope of seeing Ephraim's torch beam bobbing through the harbour as he came back with news. But all I saw was water streaming down the glass and blackness beyond. It was hard to stay hopeful, seeing that.

By the time the clock struck midnight, I couldn't bear it any more. I convinced myself the reason Ephraim hadn't returned was because he couldn't face telling me: the mission was off. They'd decided it was too dangerous to rescue anyone from northern France. It didn't take much effort to picture Sukie at gunpoint or being dragged by the Gestapo to some rat-infested prison.

Tightening the blanket around my shoulders, I couldn't get warm. If Dad were here now he'd talk to me, listen to me, make me see things in a different way.

'Dad,' I whispered out loud. 'Please make sure Sukie comes home. Seeing as you didn't, it's only fair that she does, don't you think? I don't mean to bargain, but—'

'Who are you talking to, Olive?' Cliff squinted sleepily at me from the top of the stairs.

I got up, shaking off the blanket and wrapping him in it. He was definitely ill because he didn't fidget or tell me not to fuss. Glad of the company, I made him have the chair while I perched on its arm. 'I've got something to show you,' I said.

There was an oil lamp burning brightly on a little table beside the chair. Taking Sukie's note from my pocket, I was about to explain to Cliff how the code worked, thinking he'd like to know. Yet as I held the paper up with the light behind it, something I'd not noticed before caught my eye. Very, *very* faintly you could see another mark on the paper. It wasn't much. But once you looked carefully in the right sort of light, it didn't say Day 9 at all but Day 19. Not an opposite at all.

'Cliff,' I said slowly. 'When would Day 19 be?'

'Day *19*?' He scowled. 'What you on about? It says Day 9.'

I pointed to the ink stain on the paper. It'd been made by water – the burst water mains from the air raid. It was easy to see how I'd missed it before, reading it by weak torchlight or under bedclothes. And it was pretty simple to work out, even for a maths dunderhead like me, that nineteen days had passed since the air raid.

I caught Cliff's eye. He grinned. Suddenly I was grinning too.

Day 19 was today. Tonight.

The boat wasn't stuck in France, or even delayed. It was on its way at this very moment. Everything was going to plan.

I jumped up, hands cupping my own face in excitement. 'Right! Action stations, Cliff! What do we need to do first?'

Cliff passed me the binoculars he'd brought upstairs. 'Have a look through these. There's a flashing light out to sea.'

I grabbed them. 'Where? Which window?'

Cliff pointed to the one on the left. I raced over, resting my elbows on the sill to steady them. Pressed the binoculars to my eyes.

Then. Just to the left. A bright light flashing on and off. It was there, then gone again. There, then gone. But it was most definitely a light.

This was a quiet stretch of sea, I reminded myself, my heart beating very fast. The fishing boats were still moored in the harbour: they didn't go out in a storm.

I handed the binoculars back to Cliff. 'It's got to be the boat from France, hasn't it?'

'I reckon so. Where's Ephraim? We need to tell him.'

'At Queenie's.' I fetched my coat, buttoning it up all wrong in the rush. 'You'll be okay here if I go?'

'Course.' He was already kneeling importantly in the chair nearest the window. 'I'll keep lookout.'

*

The wind was so strong it blew me like a leaf up the hill to Queenie's. No one heard me knocking on the front door so I tried the little window to the left of the steps, just like I'd done on our first night here.

'Oh come on, come *on*!' I muttered, hugging myself against the icy, sideways rain. I was impatient to be back on the beach. You could hear the sea roar, the waves thump as they hit the harbour wall. It was going to be a heck of a job landing the boat safely, and without drawing attention to ourselves. I wasn't sure how far off the coast it was, but every minute standing here we were wasting time.

I was just about to give up and try Mrs Henderson's instead when I remembered the back door. You reached it by an alley at the side of the house, and it opened on to the kitchen, where Queenie and Ephraim might well be. It had to be worth a try.

In the day the door was always open. At night, Queenie bolted it on the inside. So again, I had to knock. This time I heard the noise of a chair scraping the floor. At last someone was coming. The door, though, stayed shut.

'Who's there?' It was Esther, sounding frightened. 'What do you want?'

I was a bit taken aback. 'It's Olive. Look, is Queenie there? Or Ephraim? It's important.'

There was a grinding, snapping sound as the bolt drew back. Esther opened the door. She was wearing her nightdress with a sweater over the top. Behind her, I glimpsed a chair full of blankets pulled up close to the kitchen fire.

'I couldn't sleep,' she mumbled. 'And no, no one's here.'

'D'you know where they are? I need to find them, Esther. There's a boat coming in!'

That got her attention. 'A *what*?'

I glanced out into the street, anxious to be gone. 'A boat. There's people aboard. It's just offshore and we have to bring it in before it ends up in the quicksands.'

'I'll get my things.'

She came back moments later, coat and boots on.

'Right. Now we need to find the others. Tell them what's happening,' I said to her.

Esther looked me in the eye, boldly, directly, like someone I'd want on my side.

'I don't know where they are,' she answered. 'But Olive, we can do this. Let's bring the boat in by ourselves.'

*

Down on the beach, there was no sign of Queenie or the others. All I could see were the white tops of the waves as they crashed on to the shingle.

'What shall we do first?' Esther shouted above the wind.

'Flash your torch out to sea,' I yelled back because it seemed like a sensible idea.

Out there somewhere in the storm was Sukie. She might even be able to see us, or hear us. Though I was freezing and frightened, the thought kept me going.

It was Esther who spotted it first. 'Light! Over to the left! Coming in fast!'

My heart leaped to my throat. There was the sound of scrabbling on the shingle as Esther rushed to the water's edge. In my torch beam, I glimpsed her knee-deep in the shallows.

'Can't see anything more!' she called. 'Whatever it was has gone!'

'False alarm.' I breathed out. Almost.

'Light!' Esther screamed again. 'LIGHT! I said LIGHT!'

Sure enough, there in the blackness was a light. It was bobbing about wildly. Dropping. Rising. Dropping again. The sea was so huge we kept losing sight of it.

'They're coming in!' I yelled, straining on tiptoe. 'Over to the right – look!'

The light vanished again.

'They're heading for the rocks!' Esther cried.

'That's not rocks, that's the quicksands.'

She didn't hear me. She set off half running, half scrambling along the beach, heading straight towards the groyne.

I tried to shout: 'Wait! Don't go any further!' but the wind snatched my words away.

Wavering up ahead, I spotted the beam from Esther's torch. Thankfully, she wasn't that far away, though trying to run after her over the shingle was like wading through snowdrifts. Too quickly I grew exhausted. On my right was the sea, which helped orientate me. All the time the boat was coming closer. It was level with me now, and moving diagonally towards the shore.

'Esther, stop!' I yelled at the very top of my lungs. 'STOP!'

Her torch beam picked out the slimy black wood of the groyne. Just as she reached it, she slowed, looking over her shoulder to locate the boat; she was a little way ahead of it still. A blast of wind sent me stumbling forwards. In a few strides, I was able, at last, to reach her. I threw my arms round her waist and hung on tight.

'Don't go any further. It's quicksand!' I gasped.

Esther fell back against me. We both staggered, quickly finding our balance again. The very next wave brought the boat in close enough to hear the slap of something thrown into the water.

'Catch the rope!' Esther cried.

I got there first. Esther was right behind me. Between us we grabbed the rope and, hand over hand, started heaving. Torches flashed. I heard shouting. The roar of waves. The boat was suddenly alarmingly near, a dark shape rising out of the water.

And then it was gone again.

We still had the rope, but it was slipping all too easily from our hands. Gritting my teeth, I wrapped it round my wrist. I tried not to think of the pain.

'Hold on!' Esther yelled behind me. 'Don't let go!'

I turned to reply when a wave knocked me off my feet. My mouth, my head, was full of water, so freezing cold it burned. My hands grabbed at nothing.

'The rope!' Esther screamed, beside me now. 'Where is it?'

We were all legs and feet as we thrashed about in the surf. Then my arm jerked so hard I thought it'd be torn off. Still wrapped around my wrist was the end of the rope. With my free hand, I grabbed Esther to anchor me. And there – still there, bucking and dipping in the swell – I caught sight of lights again.

Esther, in front of me now, got both hands on the rope. I couldn't feel my fingers any more or my face. The water swirled around us, tugging at our legs, making it hard to stand upright. Harder still to pull against the waves. Alone, I'd never have managed. But somehow, between us, we dug our feet into the shingle and leaned back.

For ages it felt like we were pulling in vain. And then suddenly the boat was coming in way too fast.

'Watch out!' Esther cried.

As another massive wave shunted it on to the beach, we threw ourselves clear just in time. The bottom of the boat ground against the shingle. Someone shouted. In torch beams, I glimpsed the red painted side of a boat, what looked like an oar, a pair of legs dangling over the side.

Very quickly, people started dropping into the water. I heard voices in a language I didn't recognise; Esther did, though, and called out: '*Shalom! Shalom!*'

In moments, we were standing thigh-deep in water, arms raised, taking suitcases, grandmothers, boxes, whatever came out of the boat. There were people everywhere, some laughing in relief, some crying, some hardly able to stand.

An old man with a violin case simply sat on the beach and sobbed.

I don't know why, but I'd not expected children. There were a couple of boys Cliff's age, dazed with shock. A little girl I lifted off the boat who clung to her toy dog, a family all together who kept hugging each other and counting heads just to double-check they'd all made it. None of it seemed quite real.

Heaps of wet belongings now littered the beach. People stood in huddles, shivering, unsure what to do next. As the last of the passengers clambered off the boat,

I was aware I'd not yet spotted Sukie. There were quite a few young women in the crowd, but none was her.

'Hang on, Olive,' Esther said, as I unwound the rope from my wrist. 'There's a couple more still on board.'

The last passengers were a woman and a man. The woman was crying; it was clear she didn't want to get off the boat. She held a white bundle in her arms. The man was trying to take the bundle from her, persuading her to climb down. All the while, the boat was rocking dangerously in the surf.

As I gripped the rope again, Esther did the same. The water, now churning around the boat, was trying to drag it back out to sea. The man sensed it. Swinging himself over the side, he grabbed the woman. Somehow the pair tumbled down on to the beach.

The waves were coming in faster. The rope was taut again, pulling against us. My arms felt ready to drop off.

'What do we do now?' I yelled to Esther. 'I can't hold on much longer.'

'Can you just—'

All I could hear was water as the sea crashed over us. Coming up for air, I heard screaming. Not Esther but the woman with the white bundle, only she wasn't holding it any more. She was back in the water, desperately clawing at the side of the boat. I couldn't understand what she wanted.

'What's she saying?' I yelled to Esther. 'What's wrong?' But I saw the look of horror on Esther's face. Coming from inside the boat was a high-pitched wailing sound.

A baby.

In a blur of panic, I pulled as if Cliff's life depended on it. Other hands grabbed the rope, voices shouting. People rushed into the water, throwing themselves against the boat to stop it moving. Yet the sea kept coming, swirling and tugging, fighting to win.

I don't know how long we stood there. Time seemed to stop. The shouting became yells, then, eventually, a cheer. Inch by inch, the boat came in until it hit the beach and we couldn't move it any more. Feeling the rope slacken, I let go at last. We weren't in water any longer. Somehow, together, we'd shifted the boat so it now sat surprisingly high up the beach.

My backside hit the ground with a thud. Esther dropped down beside me, breathing like she'd run for miles. I was aware of people standing over us, asking if we were all right. And somewhere nearby, a baby still crying, but in a gentler way, and a woman's voice saying, 'Sssshhhh, Reuben, shhhh,' over and over.

I couldn't speak. I lay flat on my back, wondering if I was going to be sick. My hands felt like they were on fire, yet my feet had never been so cold.

The first voice I recognised was Queenie's. I couldn't make out where she was. Then she crouched down beside me and helped me sit up.

'You're here!' I nearly burst out crying. 'I came to fetch you. Where *were* you all?'

'At Mrs Henderson's, using her radio. Mine's extremely temperamental in bad weather.'

I tried to explain. 'The code was wrong. I mean … we weren't reading it properly—'

Queenie squeezed my shoulder. 'You've done a remarkable thing here tonight, Olive. Not only did you discover something the rest of us missed. You brought the boat in by yourself.'

'Not quite,' I replied. 'Esther and me did it together.'

In the beam of Queenie's torch, I caught Esther's eye. She almost smiled. Then, of a sudden, a look of disbelief crossed her face.

'What's the matter?' I asked.

She didn't answer. Getting very slowly to her feet, she looked dazed. Wondering if somehow she'd bumped her head, I stood up to take hold of her by the elbow. Like me she was shivering from head to toe.

'Let's go back to mine and get warm, shall we?' Queenie said, trying to move us on up the beach.

But Esther was staring – sleepwalker-staring – at a group of people not far from us. One of them, a man in a long dark coat, called out, 'Esther?'

She listened. Didn't move.

The man was coming towards her now in big, raking strides. Still she didn't move. Yet I could almost feel the air around her change. She took a step towards the man.

Then she was running. Shouting, 'Papa!' against the wind.

'Esti!' the man cried. 'Look at you! My child!'

'That's her *father*?' My mouth fell open.

'We didn't want to get her hopes up, just in case it didn't come off,' Queenie explained. 'That was why she couldn't live with Ephraim. It's much easier to keep it secret in a big house with a cellar.'

I was only half listening, unable to take my eyes off Esther and her father. I let myself – just for a moment – imagine it was *my* dad who'd miraculously turned up. *My* dad hugging *me*. I could feel Esther's joy like it was real. And actually, it was. Knowing what it was like to lose my dad, I was just so thankful she'd been reunited with hers.

It's a Full-time Job to Win

We now had to get everyone quickly and quietly off the beach.

'Here, carry these, will you?' Miss Carter thrust a bundle of clothes into my arms. 'We're taking everyone to Queenie's. Torches off. We don't want to attract attention.'

There were thirty-two refugees in total: thirty-two wet, frightened, exhausted people, who'd travelled through a storm in a sailing boat meant to hold ten. How awful their lives back home must've been to take such a risk.

And these weren't fighters or soldiers, but the sort of people you'd walk past every day in the street: men with grey hair, a girl and her brother holding hands, two old ladies whose dripping wet glasses kept sliding down their noses. Baby Reuben, now safely wrapped in his blanket again, back in his mother's arms. But, to my growing concern, there was no sign of a pretty seventeen-year-old girl amongst them.

Mrs Henderson seemed to be looking for someone too: 'I've not seen her yet,' she was saying to Queenie. 'I'd recognise her from her picture, I'm sure I would.'

Following the crowd along the beach, I caught up with Ephraim. He was carrying a bedroll under one arm, a suitcase in the other.

'Have you seen Sukie?' I asked him.

'She's not here, Olive.' He sounded irritated. 'So she can't be involved, can she?'

'She must be,' I insisted. 'She had the code.'

In frustration, he raised his shoulders skywards. 'I don't know what's happened, all right? A mix-up? An accident? All I know is she's not here, so stop asking.'

*

Back at Queenie's her kitchen was bright, warm and soon very full of people peeling off wet coats and thawing their hands by the fire. It was a completely different room to how I'd remembered it on our first night here. Something was actually cooking on the stove and the table was laden with plates, bowls, spoons and loaves of bread.

'Welcome, everyone,' Mrs Henderson announced,

clearing her throat. 'Or should I say *Shalom*? Forgive my rusty Hebrew, please, eat all you can.'

Thick carrot soup was ladled on to plates and into bowls, and when they ran out, into cups. With each serving, Queenie also gave out envelopes, which people seemed equally grateful for. They were, Miss Carter told me, fake identity papers.

'We need it to look official,' she explained. 'On their own papers, these people wouldn't be allowed into our country, sadly.'

'So they're staying here for just a few days?' I asked, remembering what Queenie had told me.

'Only until they're strong enough to travel on. We'll try to keep it as low-key as possible, but you know what this place is like – someone's bound to stick their beak in, somehow.'

Yet the mood in Queenie's kitchen right now was joyful, almost giddy, like that of a birthday tea or a Christmas dinner. We'd been part of something no one had expected to succeed and against the odds it had. Yet for me it felt bittersweet because Sukie wasn't there, so I was glad to be kept busy, slicing bread, offering refills of soup.

'You'll have heard the news?' Mrs Henderson sidled up to Miss Carter, who was next to me cutting more bread. 'Our contact didn't make it on to the boat.'

I stopped slicing to listen.

'No, no,' said Mrs Henderson quickly, keen to dispel the concern on Miss Carter's face. 'We've had no reports of a casualty. Apparently, she ran off as the boat was leaving. They couldn't wait. They had to sail without her.'

Miss Carter looked shocked. 'How very odd. I thought Mrs Arby was one of the best.'

Mrs Arby: that name again. The contact from London who everyone trusted, but no one seemed to have met. I watched as Miss Carter threaded her way across the room to break the news to Ephraim and Queenie. Their reactions were similar – a nod, a shake of the head, a look of disbelief – as if they'd expected better from their mysterious Mrs Arby.

After the initial relief, the mood in the room grew quieter, more thoughtful. Some of the refugees had already fallen asleep in their seats, Ephraim's hand-knitted socks warming their feet. Little Reuben was snoring heartily. His mum, a lady called Miriam, let me hold him for a moment, and I marvelled at his tiny pink fingers and the jet-black curls on his head.

'He's so little,' I murmured.

'Isn't he?' Miriam spoke perfect English. 'He's only five days old, you know.'

And theirs wasn't the only incredible story. By the fire, a brother and sister – Jakob and Elise – played cards like normal families did. Except their parents had been sent to a camp in Poland, and they'd only escaped a similar fate after a sympathetic doctor hid them both by strapping them to the underside of a stretcher, then carrying them into a waiting ambulance.

Mrs Henderson told me all this. And really, it was quite a lot to take in. We also managed to track down the rightful owner of the waterlogged suitcase, a small, dark-haired woman called Judith. Ephraim said he'd go back to the lighthouse to fetch it for her. I asked him to check on Cliff while he was there.

'We hit a huge wave yesterday and it fell overboard.' She spoke in German which Queenie translated. 'It's a miracle it turned up on this beach – a sign we were meant to come here.'

I wanted to hear more of her story, but by now there was a mountain of washing-up to do, and Mrs Henderson was bustling me towards the sink.

'Let's make a start on these dishes,' she ordered. 'I'll wash, you dry.'

The sight of all the dirty plates made me suddenly

aware of how exhausted I was. It was the middle of the night, after all. But as we worked, we got talking some more about the refugees and I soon forgot to be tired.

They were mostly from Austria, Mrs Henderson told me, all Jewish but for one young woman – a ballerina – whose Romany parents had been put in prison by the Nazis. She was called Lyuba Zingari, which I thought a marvellous name, and was trying to get to America to become a famous dancer.

'Hitler's persecuting the Roma people too,' Mrs Henderson explained. 'It's dreadful. I often wonder where it will all end.'

Amongst the Jews were Mr Geffen, a concert violinist; a writer called Mr Krauss who'd travelled with his mother; the Schoenman family who made puppets from scrap cloth and string. Their three daughters, Rosa, Anna and Mimi, could play just about any musical instrument you could name.

'That Mimi Schoenman.' Mrs Henderson pointed a soapy finger at a tall, pale girl with startling green eyes. 'She sings like one of God's own angels, so I'm told.'

The other refugees were librarians, a baker, three men who wrote for newspapers, a singer, a shopkeeper, and two young women who were teachers, called Fräulein Weber and Frau Berliner. Hearing their stories made me sadder, somehow, because these people weren't strangers any more – they had names, did important jobs, had exciting futures ahead. One of them was only five days old.

Like the people in that miserable newsreel, they all had yellow badges sewn on to the left breast of their coats. They were star-shaped, the word *Jude* written in handwriting clumsier than Cliff's. They weren't badges to be proud of like the ones we got at school for good work. Their only purpose, it seemed, was to make sure people knew: *you* were one of those 'types' Hitler loathed.

How could these people be made to feel ashamed of who they were? I hadn't thought I could hate the Nazis more than I already did. Now, though, I really understood why Sukie was so distraught at what was happening in Europe. We weren't Jewish, but we were human beings and that was more than enough reason to be outraged.

'Look at those two,' Mrs Henderson said, nodding in the direction of Esther and her dad.

I let out a long breath. It was hard *and* lovely seeing them nestled against each other, like they fitted, somehow. My dad gave hugs like that too. It was odd – and rather comforting – to think it was something Esther and me had in common.

Mrs Henderson handed me another soapy plate. 'Esther's father's a doctor. He's called Dr Wirth.'

'So is that Esther's real surname?' I asked.

'The Jenkins family, who took her in after the Kindertransport, gave her their surname. She didn't expect to see any of her family again. This was supposed to be a fresh start for her, here in England. Her mother, God bless her, was already dead. Her father was in trouble with the authorities.'

'For doing what?' Though I had pretty much guessed the answer: he was Jewish.

'It's just so *stupid*,' I said, drying the plate rather roughly. 'How can you hate someone just because of how they live their life?'

Mrs Henderson sighed. 'People like to have something to hate – it makes life easier when things go wrong if there's someone to blame. Think about what happened here today with that pilot, Olive.'

She meant how quickly the crowd turned on him. It was frightening how easily normal, pleasant people got whipped up into nastiness. The possibility that something similar had happened to Esther's family disturbed me.

'But it's worse than that, isn't it?' I said, thinking. 'The German pilot was a fighter from the enemy side.

Esther's family were ... well ... just *people*.'

'Yes, my dear,' Mrs Henderson sighed again, blowing damp strands of hair off her face. 'Normal, educated, cultured people. It was all very well, the Kindertransport, but what good's a child without its parents? You saw what it did to Esther.'

'Well, I'm glad they're all here,' I said. 'I'm glad you helped them.'

Mrs Henderson looked sad. 'But we can't save everyone ... our government needs to take some responsibility and do much, *much* more. We should be helping them flee Hitler, not turning them away. We've had to smuggle these good people in like criminals.'

*

That night Mrs Henderson took in ten refugees. Queenie kept the rest at the post office, where beds were made up on whatever mattresses and chairs could be found. It was daybreak when the house finally quietened down.

'You look done in,' Ephraim said, handing me my coat. 'I'll finish up here. You go on to bed.'

The sink was full of dirty plates again but I was too tired to argue. And I felt bad for leaving Cliff, who I'd barely given a second thought to all night.

After the heat and noise of Queenie's, it was nice just to be outside. It wasn't raining any more. The storm had passed, leaving the air salt-sharp, and the gulls shrieking like they did after bad weather. At the sides of the street, the gutters were full of shingle blown in from the beach. Everything else – cobbles, roof tiles, windows – glistened like it'd all been scrubbed clean.

It was hard to believe so much had happened in just a few hours. All at once I felt a bit overcome and started to cry, quietly, to myself.

'Olive?' Someone called. 'Wait a second, will you?'

Turning, I saw Miss Carter hurrying down the street. I wiped my face with my hand and smiled wearily. 'Did I forget my hat?'

'No.' She stopped in front of me. 'Ephraim told me you had an idea that your sister might've been on the boat?'

I gave a little shrug.

'I'm sure your sister is a marvellous girl,' she said, her hand gentle on my arm. 'But she's not involved in any of this. She never has been.'

I welled up again and tried staring at the ground. At Miss Carter's feet in their large, immaculate leather brogues.

'She's gone missing, though,' I muttered dismally.

'And she had a coded note in her pocket, but no one seems to know how it got there.'

Miss Carter sighed patiently. 'Look, I can see you're upset, and I understand. But you have to be realistic, I'm afraid. Your sister must've disappeared off somewhere else. Did she have a boyfriend, perhaps?'

'Ephraim,' I stated.

'Oh.' Miss Carter seemed taken aback. 'Right . . . I didn't know.'

'Sukie hated Hitler and wanted to help people, and the night she went missing she did meet a man, but he didn't seem like a boyfriend . . .'

Staring at Miss Carter's hair, cut short at the neck I fell silent. She was tall, wore glasses. It struck me that she could – in the right clothes, from a distance – pass as a man.

Perhaps she saw the realisation in my face. For suddenly something seemed to click in her brain too and she narrowed her eyes at my coat.

'No,' she said, shaking her head. 'That's impossible.'

'What is?'

She didn't answer. Backing away from me and breaking into a run, she disappeared up the street.

COUGHS AND SNEEZES
SPREAD DISEASES

Cliff was just waking up as I got in.

'Is Sukie here?' he asked.

Desperate as I was to fall into my bed I sat on his, trying to decide what to tell him. Sukie hadn't arrived and it seemed I was the only one who'd expected her to. Yet no one could explain why she'd had the coded note, and now, to top it all, Miss Carter was acting strangely.

'Did the Jewish people come too?' Cliff peered at me, bleary-eyed.

'Yes,' I replied, happier to talk about this. 'They made it, and you'll never guess what, but Esther's dad was with them. She's completely over the moon.' I told him about the ballerina with the lovely name and the family who made puppets and the old ladies with rain-splattered glasses.

Cliff shut his eyes again. 'Really? Sounds nice.' He

didn't seem to be listening any more.

It concerned me that he wasn't getting better. If anything this morning he seemed worse.

'Is your belly button still hurting?' I asked.

'The pain's here now.' His hand hovered over his right side. Suddenly he tried to sit up. 'Quick! I'm going to be sick!'

I found our chamber pot just in time. Poor Pixie didn't like the retching sounds and hid under the bed.

'You need to see a doctor,' I told him, when he'd finished. 'As soon as Ephraim gets home we're taking you. And that's an order.'

Luckily, Ephraim was back within half an hour. After wrapping Cliff in a blanket, we realised he was too ill to even stand.

'Right.' Ephraim braced himself. 'Let's get him down.'

I watched in horror as he heaved Cliff on to his shoulders. It was exactly how he carried Pixie down the ladder. I didn't think I could bear to watch.

'Shouldn't we get the doctor to come here?' I asked anxiously.

But Ephraim already had one foot on the ladder. Pixie, cross at being left behind, whined and scratched at the front door. What with that and Cliff's groaning, I was very glad when we made it safely on to the ground.

'Try not to cry,' I told Cliff, giving him a quick hug. 'You'll soon be better.' He really didn't look good, though.

Between us, Ephraim and me carried him out of the harbour and up the hill. Cliff wasn't heavy exactly, but we were trying to hurry and at the same time not hurt him, so it was arm-achingly awkward.

At last, we turned towards the church. The house just before it – red-brick, severe-looking – was Dr Morrison's. His housekeeper showed us into a stuffy room that smelled of cigars. Very gently, we lowered Cliff on to a chair. The pain nearly made him pass out. When the doctor joined us, he was still chewing what I guessed was a mouthful of his breakfast. He looked in a hurry to get back to it too.

One by one, I reeled off Cliff's symptoms. It was quite a list – in normal circumstances, my brother would've been rather impressed.

'There's a nasty stomach upset doing the rounds,' Dr Morrison told us. 'I suggest you take him home and put him to bed.'

I stared at him in surprise. 'Aren't you going to examine him?'

'Examine him?' the doctor said tetchily. 'My dear, I can spot a stomach upset at fifty paces.'

Out in the street, I couldn't contain my anger. 'A stomach bug? What twaddle! I bet he doesn't treat his local patients like this!'

Cliff was getting worse before our eyes. Even breathing seemed to hurt him now.

'What the heck should we do?' I was beginning to despair.

'There's a woman in the next village who uses herbs,' Ephraim offered.

Herbs?

'Blimey, it was just a suggestion,' Ephraim muttered, reading my expression.

'What about Dr Wirth?' I said, suddenly. Queenie's – where we'd find him – was just a few doors down the street.

*

Dr Wirth was in Queenie's kitchen, discussing with Esther how best to wind up the stopped clock. One look at Cliff and the doctor got to his feet.

'I'll wash my hands,' he said.

While Dr Wirth prodded Cliff and listened to what Ephraim told him, I slipped into a seat opposite Esther. She didn't speak or smile or do anything pally. But things did feel different between us, like we'd accepted each other's right to exist.

'This young man needs an operation urgently,' Dr Wirth said, once he'd finished his examination. He had the same slightly husky accent as Esther. 'His appendix is about to rupture, and if that happens...' He made a horrible exploding gesture with his hands.

I wished Mum was here.

'Where's the nearest hospital?' Dr Wirth asked.

'Plymouth,' said Ephraim. 'About twenty miles away.'

'We must get him there as quickly as we can.'

*

Mrs Henderson, it turned out, knew a goat farmer with a van. In next to no time, a tall, robust man, called Mr Fairweather arrived, and in one swoop hoisted Cliff out of his chair.

'You weigh no more than my best Anglo-Nubian, you don't,' he said cheerfully. He'd put fresh straw down in the back of his van, and a clean bucket: 'In case your guts don't hold, lad,' Mr Fairweather told Cliff. His kindness made me want to weep.

As I went to climb into the van beside Cliff,

Ephraim stopped me. 'He'll need an adult with him at the hospital. I'll go.'

'I can't leave him,' I protested.

'You've done your bit, Olive. Now let the doctors do theirs.'

Frustrated, I felt myself welling up. 'He's my brother. He needs me. He'll be frightened on his own,' though he probably wouldn't with Ephraim looking after him.

'Hurry up, you two,' Mr Fairweather called from the driver's seat.

'Take care of Pixie for me.' Ephraim got into the van before I could argue any more. 'I'll let Queenie know any news. Try not to worry.'

I stepped back on to the pavement, defeated.

Yet watching the van disappear up the street was almost a relief. I couldn't do any more. I couldn't help Cliff get better, nor could I make Sukie appear on a boat. I felt overwhelmingly tired. All I wanted was Mum to smooth my hair off my forehead and tell me everything would be fine.

Back inside, Queenie was about to open the shop for business. I'd expected her to be dead on her feet like me, but she was humming a tune under her breath. and her eyes were twinkling, almost smiling.

'I need to send an urgent telegram to London,

please,' I said, trying hard not to stare.

Taking a form from a drawer, Queenie passed it to me with a pen. 'Keep it brief,' she instructed. 'You pay by the word.'

In the 'message goes here' box, I wrote:

This Form must accompany any inquiry made respecting this Telegram.

POST OFFICE TELEGRAPHS.

Office Stamp

If the Receiver of an Inland Telegram doubts its accuracy, he may have it repeated on payment of half the amount originally paid for its transmission, any fraction of 1d, less than ½ d, being reckoned as 1/d d; and if it be found that there was any inaccuracy, the amount paid for repetition will be refunded. Special conditions are applicable to the repetition of Foreign Telegrams.

Handed in at   Office of Origin and Service Instructions.

Charges to pay

£ s.d

Words

Received here at

Cliff in hospital Stop Appendix trouble Stop Please come at once Stop
Olive

Mum arrived from Paddington on the 4.30 p.m. express. I went to the station to meet her, taking Pixie, who needed the walk. Throwing my arms around Mum's neck, I breathed in her familiar lily of the valley smell and felt relieved.

'Gosh, what a welcome!' Mum stepped back

anxiously. 'Is there any more news? I telephoned the hospital before I left and Cliff was just going to theatre.'

'He's fine,' I reassured her. 'Ephraim just called to say he's in recovery. He's allowed one visitor tomorrow.' We both knew that visitor would be Mum.

It was a shock to see how thin she'd got since we'd said our goodbyes just over two weeks ago. She'd put on her make-up more heavily than usual; it didn't suit her. I wondered if I'd done the right thing, bringing her all this way when she still wasn't well. But it was too late to worry about that.

'This is Pixie,' I explained, trying to cheer things up. The little dog did her best, the dear thing, squirming in delight and rolling over for a tummy tickle.

Mum smiled. 'She's adorable.'

'Cliff loves her. He'll be wanting his own dog when we come home.'

'We'll see.' Straightening up from stroking Pixie, Mum narrowed her eyes at me. 'You're not sleeping, are you? You look tired.'

'So do you, Mum,' I replied.

Slipping my arm through hers, I took her to Queenie's, which was closest, and told her all about Dr Wirth as we walked.

At Queenie's, Mum insisted on shaking Dr Wirth by the hand.

'I cannot thank you enough for what you did for my boy,' she gushed. 'Olive tells me you saved his life.'

'Kindness repays kindness,' he replied. And he gave her a very sincere handshake in return, holding her hand in both of his, which made Mum go rather red-faced for some reason.

As I organised some tea, the kitchen became busy. Mr Geffen the violinist joined us at the table, then Miss Zingari, the ballerina, who insisted on pouring our tea and handing round the biscuits. Anna and Rosa Schoenman told Mum, in faltering English, that they'd made up a play with puppets about their journey and would she like to watch? Mum looked genuinely delighted – and it was lovely, if a little unexpected, to have such a warm welcome.

A quick, cheery knock at the back door announced Miss Carter's arrival. 'Hullo! Is Queenie here? I'm just ... Oh!' The sight of Mum made her visibly jump.

'We meet at last,' Mum said coolly, putting down her teacup.

'You're here!' Miss Carter gasped. 'How?'

'By the Paddington train.'

Miss Carter seemed a bit thrown. So was I by her reaction: it was certainly odd.

'It's a great honour,' Miss Carter said hurriedly. 'You look just like your photograph.'

My confusion grew as she came into the kitchen and, wiping her palm on her slacks, went to shake Mum's hand; Mum didn't take it.

'Oh.' Miss Carter withdrew her hand.

It was horribly awkward. I liked Miss Carter, who'd always been nice to me, and couldn't understand why Mum was being so rude. I wasn't the only one who'd noticed, either. Dr Wirth, getting up from the table, gestured to the other refugees that it was time to leave the room. As the door closed behind them, the kitchen became ominously quiet.

'Do you two know each other?' I asked warily.

'Yes.' They both said it at the exact same time.

I glanced at Mum, who seemed suddenly fierce. In contrast Miss Carter looked terrified. Something was definitely going on between them. The only connection I could think of was Sukie.

Now I was nervous. '*How* do you know each other, exactly?'

'Through work,' Miss Carter said. 'Though we

haven't met in person until now. It's rather sensitive, the work we do, so the fewer the better.'

I didn't understand what she was saying. Mum worked in the printworks in Whitechapel; she'd done so for ages.

'But Miss Carter helps rescue refugees,' I pointed out to Mum.

'Yes,' Mum replied. 'She does.'

She spread her hands on the table, where I could see they were trembling.

'Miss Carter,' she said. 'Why don't you pull up a chair?'

Reluctantly, Miss Carter sat across the table from Mum. She fiddled with an empty teacup, unable to look either of us in the eye. It came to me again, in a rush. Miss Carter was the 'man' my sister met, wasn't she?

'You gave Sukie the note that night, didn't you?' I said outright.

For a moment, I thought Miss Carter was going to deny it. Then her face crumpled and she burst into tears.

'I made a terrible error. It was too dark, that night, too wet. I read the code wrong and told everyone here the wrong date, didn't I?' she sobbed, taking off her glasses. 'This stupid mess is all my fault.'

In that moment I didn't know whether to hug her or hate her. Because of her mistake, my sister was missing. But I sensed there was more.

'Who's this Mrs Arby you all keep talking about?' I demanded. 'Were you supposed to give the note to her?'

Mum blinked. 'Mrs Arby?' She said it differently to the others – not 'Arby', with the stress at the start of the name, but 'RB', like initials.

I stared at her.

RB.

It was obvious. Sukie, dressed in Mum's coat, with her hair styled glamorously, looked older – old enough to pass for Mrs Rachel Bradshaw. In the chaos of the air raid, it'd been an easy mistake to make, getting a person's identity wrong. Which meant the mysterious Mrs Arby, the London contact who everyone trusted, who'd done jobs like this before, was Rachel Bradshaw.

My mum.

WHERE SKILL AND
COURAGE COUNT

Mum got straight to the point. 'I need to clear a few things up, Olive.'

After asking Miss Carter to give us a moment alone, she told me her side of the story. I felt as if I was listening to Mrs Henderson again, hearing about the lives of people I didn't know. Only this was my own mother.

Every Monday and Friday night, leaving us with awful suppers to reheat, our mum didn't work late shifts at the printworks. She went to an office in Shoreditch. And from there, by radio, by note, by telephone and letters, she exchanged messages with Miss Carter and Mrs Henderson and Queenie and others like them on what she called 'humanitarian war work'. She'd never met any of them in person.

'I can't tell you any more details. It's secret work.

How you know even this much is really quite beyond me,' she admitted.

'I worked most of it out myself,' I told her. She might've hidden it from me all this time, but I wasn't stupid. 'Sounds like Sukie did too.'

'Your sister spied on me,' Mum replied bitterly. 'She stole paperwork, listened in to private conversations. She was very foolish to get caught up in something she knew nothing about.'

'She *did* know about it, though. What Hitler's doing really got to her. She was desperate to do something about it. All that post from Devon? It wasn't from Queenie. Those were letters from the lighthouse, written by Ephraim, who feels the same about the Jewish people as Sukie does.'

'It was stupid, impulsive behaviour,' Mum argued, 'of the sort your sister's very good at.'

Yet to me she had missed a vital point.

'You know Sukie wanted to help *you*, don't you? She saw how ill you'd got over Dad. By standing in for you on this job, she was making sure you'd get some rest, like the doctor said you should.'

'I might've known you'd stick up for your sister,' Mum remarked. 'But it didn't help me – it worried me sick!'

'It did help thirty-two refugees, though,' I reminded her.

'She was lucky she didn't get arrested straight away,' Mum went on as if she hadn't heard me. 'When I found out that night what she'd done, I was all for going after her, hauling her back and locking her in her bedroom, till this frightful war was over if I had to. But it was too late by then. She was already halfway to France.'

'You knew the *night* she disappeared?' I couldn't believe what I was hearing. 'Why didn't you tell me?'

'And admit that I do undercover work and Sukie was doing it too?' Mum cried. 'Good grief, Olive, it's secret business. It was too dangerous to tell you. There's a war on, remember!'

'People always use that excuse,' I muttered.

It stunned me that Mum had known all this time. But then, hadn't there been signs? The looks in our kitchen between her and Gloria, the refusal to talk about Sukie, the bundling us off out of the way – to here, the very place Sukie might, with any luck, show up. It was a clever way of making sure we knew the moment she set foot on British soil again.

Mum leaned forwards, elbows on the table. She looked strong, determined, and so very much like Sukie it made my chest hurt.

'Some things *have* to be secret, don't you see? Yes, it upsets people. But it's done for good reason – to keep *even more* people safe.'

'But—'

'No buts, Olive,' Mum said firmly. 'That's the harsh reality.'

'You lied to us.'

'I did it to protect you!' she cried, sitting back in her seat. Reaching into her jacket pocket, she pulled out the postcard I'd sent her, white and tatty and covered in my big handwriting. 'I suppose this was the truth, was it?'

'It's not the same,' I said crossly.

Putting it back in her pocket, Mum reached across the table for my hand. 'I knew you'd be homesick down here, darling. I knew you were heartbroken over Dad and upset about Sukie. But you wrote this stupidly happy message to protect me, didn't you?'

I thought of the postcard, written yesterday, that I hadn't sent, and sniffed. 'Maybe. It's still not the same, though.'

'I know that.' She rubbed my knuckles gently with her thumb. 'But it might help you understand why I did it.'

I looked at her properly then, drinking in this person I thought I knew so well. Even the familiar bits – the chocolate brown eyes, the dark wavy hair – looked different somehow.

What surprised me most was the pride I had for my mum. These past months I'd seen her become a sad person who cried too much. Yet, even then, there were parts to her that were stronger than I'd ever imagined. Thinking over all she'd done, how Queenie and Ephraim and the others held her in such high regard, and how she'd inspired Sukie, I began to *feel* different too. The uneasiness that she wasn't well was still there. Mixed in with it, though, was the belief that she'd recover. I supposed what I was feeling was hope.

*

What this meant was that Sukie was the person left behind in France. When Queenie heard about Mum she apologised for not believing me.

'You were right about your sister. I should've listened,' she said.

Mrs Henderson, though, went bananas, storming round to Miss Carter's and blaming her to her face. Ephraim, typically, said nothing. He went to work as normal, spending long hours up in the control room, the only obvious differences being the radio was less busy and there were no sounds of knitting.

No one, including me, knew what we were going to do about Sukie.

*

The next morning Mum went to Plymouth to be with Cliff. She was planning on staying there till he was well enough to come home. Alone again, I had plenty of time to think, though the best medicine for it was to keep busy. At night, I'd read far later than usual, hoping that when I switched off my torch I'd fall asleep more easily: it didn't often work. In the day, I delivered food from Ephraim's cupboards to the refugees.

On such a morning, a few days after Mum had left, I ran into Esther in the street. She said she was going to school.

'What, now?' Our afternoon session went on long enough; I couldn't imagine anyone choosing to spend a whole day in lessons.

'Yes, *now*,' Esther said, like I was being really slow. 'Mr Barrowman's giving a talk to the local kids about the refugees.'

'I thought the plan was to keep things low-profile.'

'Too late for that,' Esther replied.

Actually, I was glad someone was addressing the issue. What had started out as a low-key mission had quickly become the talk of the village. There weren't thirty-two refugees any more – Miss Zingari had already gone to catch a ship to New York, and a few of the others had taken trains to London. Yet the word soon got round that twenty or so people remained, which in a place as small as Budmouth Point was bound to stir things up.

And it had. Some of the locals had been nice. We'd had offers of clothes and food and spare beds. But plenty had been pretty hostile.

'We don't want their sort round here,' I overheard a woman in the queue at the baker's saying.

Her friend agreed. 'They won't eat our meat, so Mrs Drummond says. And they've got other funny ways you wouldn't imagine!'

It even got to the point where some people were calling Miss Carter and Mrs Henderson names in the street and boycotting Queenie's shop.

'We'd better hurry, then,' I said to Esther. 'We don't want to miss what Mr Barrowman's got to say.' Linking arms, we walked on up the street. I didn't make a big thing of it, but it was the first time I'd properly felt like her friend.

*

The school sounded hushed, like it did when lessons were in full swing.

'This way.' I beckoned Esther to the side of the building.

She looked unimpressed. 'Aren't we just going in?'

'We haven't been invited,' I reminded her.

The big window that had broken when the stray bomb fell still hadn't been fixed. If we stood right underneath it we'd hear what was going on inside. Almost straight away I recognised Mr Barrowman's voice with its London accent.

'Refugees are people who've had to flee for their lives. They're leaving their jobs, homes, families because of war. We should be welcoming them, not treating them like enemies.'

The class grumbled disagreeably.

Esther looked worried. 'Oh dear. He's laying it on a bit thick, isn't he?'

'He's *trying* to help,' I pointed out, thinking perhaps he was quite decent for a teacher after all.

'But he's stirring things up, not calming them down. My father and the others just need a few days to recover and they'll be on their way again.'

'Are you leaving as well?' I wasn't sure I liked the idea. 'Can't you all stay here in England?'

Esther shrugged. 'I don't know. The laws on asylum are so strict now, my father and the others are pretty sure they won't get accepted that way.'

'They've got identity papers.'

'Fake ones, with English names and occupations, just to get them to the nearest port and on to another boat. It's all very risky.'

The risk lay with Queenie too, then: she'd probably go to prison if she got caught forging papers. This bothered me as well.

Inside, Mr Barrowman was still talking.

'... What the Nazis are doing is terrifying. All because being Jewish doesn't fit with their ideals ...'

'My mum says them new people are Germans,' a boy interrupted, 'and you expect us to look after them.'

'They're from *Austria*,' Mr Barrowman corrected him calmly. 'A country invaded by Hitler.'

'Why should we help the Jews?' said someone else. 'What've they ever done for us?'

As the class went quiet, Mr Barrowman tried again: 'Put it another way, how would you feel if your life was at risk just because you were from Devon?'

'He can't help that, sir. He was born here,' someone

quipped. The group erupted into laughter.

'That's exactly my point. Would you stay here and die, or would you leave?'

The boy didn't respond.

'How would you feel about being spat at in the street? Or seeing your parents arrested though they'd done nothing wrong?'

I glanced nervously at Esther. Her face was tight with emotion. Perhaps listening in hadn't been such a great idea.

'This is why we're at war with Hitler. We don't hate the German people, we hate fascism. Wouldn't it be a way of letting Hitler win if we all started behaving as he does?'

It made perfect sense to me. I was expecting the class to think so too but what followed was an uncomfortable silence. A few coughs. Someone muttered about his ruler being taken. Another boy said he didn't have it.

'Yes you have, Clutterbuck. I saw you nick it.'

'Go chase yourself,' the boy snarled.

The class's usual teacher, Mrs Simmons, clapped for quiet. It was too late. By then Mr Barrowman's moment was lost.

Esther didn't stay to hear any more. I went after her

and found her sitting on the school wall, angry tears in her eyes.

'I came to England to try to forget what happened.' Esther wiped her face clumsily with her coat sleeve. 'But I can't escape it. Seeing Papa again, it's brought it all back to me.'

'Here.' Giving her my rather grubby hankie, I hopped up to sit beside her.

She took it and blew her nose. 'I know Mr Barrowman means well and I'm grateful. But . . .' She paused. 'It's *my* story, you know? I should be the one telling it.'

We sat staring out over the village to the grey-green sea, and the lighthouse, painted dull as a chimney pot.

'You can tell me if you like,' I said quietly.

I honestly didn't expect her to. And she didn't say anything for such a long time, when she did speak it surprised me.

'I can't remember a specific time when the comments and the name-calling started, but one evening in November it all got much worse,' she said. 'My brother Tobias and me were doing our homework at the dining-room table like we always did.'

'You've got a brother?'

She hesitated before nodding. 'Papa was working late

at the clinic in a friend's back room – it was against the law for Jews to work as doctors. Mama was making supper in the kitchen, and I remember her cursing because she'd just burned her hand on the griddle. Tobias and me couldn't stop laughing because Mama *never* swore.' The memory of it made her mouth twitch in an almost-smile.

'Then someone banged on our front door. It was late – too late for social calling. Mama told us not to answer it. Everyone knew someone who'd had a knock at the door like that.'

'Who was it?'

'The police, usually. Sometimes Hitler's soldiers. It was never for a good reason, and it never ended happily. We all dreaded it happening to us. So, Mama turned the lights out and put her hand over the dog's nose.' Esther, glancing sideways at me, explained: 'We had a sausage dog called Gerta who barked at everything.

'The knocking went on and they started shouting through the letter box, saying they'd burn the house down if we didn't answer the door. Mama told us to hide under the table and went to speak to them. They wanted Papa. They said he'd been treating non-Jewish patients at the clinic and it had to stop. Mama told them he wasn't here but they didn't believe her and came in anyway. There were four of them in Nazi uniform, stomping through our house in their filthy great boots. Finding us hiding under the table, they decided to take Tobias as a substitute for Papa. "When your husband hands himself in, we'll release the boy," was what they said.

'It was cold outside – a freezing Austrian winter's night – but they wouldn't let Tobias fetch his coat. As soon as they laid hands on him, Mama started screaming. She let go of Gerta and grabbed Tobias – we both did – pulling on his arms, yelling that they couldn't take him, that he'd done nothing wrong. Gerta was barking. I saw one of the men swing his boot at her. She went flying across the room, hitting the mantelpiece. It was awful. She didn't bark after that.'

It took a moment for the horror of what she was saying to sink in.

'Don't tell me any more if you don't want to,' I said gently.

She stared straight ahead like she hadn't heard me. 'They took my brother anyway. He was ten years old.

'We ran into the street after them, and it was chaos – like the end of the world or something. The whole town was full of Nazi uniforms. There were broken windows, burning houses, people sobbing in the gutter.

The synagogue at the end of our street was on fire. I was terrified. So terrified I couldn't move. But Mum kept running. Shouting and yelling and running after my brother. I didn't see what happened but I heard the gunshot.'

She stopped. Rubbed her face in her hands. 'Afterwards they gave it a very pretty name: *Kristallnacht* – meaning "the night of broken glass". But it was the night I lost my mother and my brother. I was sent away soon after as part of the Kindertransport, though Papa never got used to losing us all at once. Nor did I. That's why he came to find me. He always promised he'd try.'

Anything I might've said stayed stuck in my throat. There weren't words for it, not really. So I put my arm through Esther's and we sat, gazing out to sea, two old enemies who were, at last, friends. She was right – it was her story to tell. And I could think of plenty who might benefit from hearing it.

MAY YOU NEVER KNOW WHAT IT MEANS TO BE A REFUGEE

What happened next – *almost* next – I can only describe as miraculous. Esther Wirth had an idea that didn't involve her big mouth or her fists. Instead, it called for sewing. I confess I was so taken aback I had to ask her to repeat it when she told me.

'What you said about telling my story,' she said. 'It's got me thinking.'

We were at the lighthouse, having tea. When I'd invited her, Esther had shrugged and said, 'Why not?' quite casually. Yet once she saw the lighthouse ladder we had to climb and the lovely rooms inside, her whole face lit up into the hugest of smiles. She was a dab hand at making toast too. We ate a big pile of it topped with Ephraim's crab-apple jam, and made Pixie beg for the crusts. It was the nicest tea I'd had in ages.

'We'll ask if we can borrow the refugees' coats

tomorrow,' Esther explained, wiping crumbs from her mouth.

'What for?'

'You've seen the badges?' She meant the yellow stars with *Jude* on them, which meant 'Jew' in German. 'They left in such a hurry, some people didn't get the chance to remove them. It's time they came off. And I've an idea who's going to do it.'

*

The next morning being a school day meant we'd find the local kids in class. Bright and early, we visited all the refugees, rounding up more coats than we could sensibly carry. By the time we reached school, my arms were ready to drop off, but we kept going until we arrived at the classroom door.

'What now?' I asked Esther, since neither of us had a free hand to knock.

Esther did that one thing Mum said girls should never do: she winked. Then pushing down with her elbow on the handle, she managed to open the door.

Mrs Simmons, the teacher, shrieked in surprise. 'Good gracious!'

It must've been a bit of a shock, to be fair. We were

little more than two enormous piles of coats, with legs sticking out the bottom. Unable to hold on to mine any more, I placed them as gently as I could on the floor. Straightening up again, I got my first full view of the class: twenty Budmouth Point kids staring right back at us. My mouth turned dry. Without really meaning to, I edged nearer to the door. Esther had no such qualms. Only this time, instead of squaring up to the local children, she laid out her father's coat on the front desk.

'I don't know what you think you're doing,' Mrs Simmons said shrilly. 'But you're not doing it in my classroom.'

Taking Esther's arm, she tried steering her towards the exit. Esther dug her heels in, and I blocked the way. Thinking it all good entertainment, the Budmouth kids started slow clapping and cheering. Already, we were more interesting than their geometry lesson, and we hadn't yet said a word.

At the second attempt, Esther managed to display the coat properly, holding it by the shoulders so everyone got a good view of the yellow star.

'I'm going to fetch the headmaster,' Mrs Simmons spluttered, but didn't leave the room.

Bit by bit, the noise died away. The pupils began to

look quite intrigued. Some sat forward, chins in hands. You could see the mockery still lingering in their faces like they were waiting for something to make fun of. But as Esther explained the yellow stars and what they meant, their expressions changed.

It was like watching newspaper catch light when you made a fire. Once it took hold, the flames began to spread and glow. At last, the class were starting to understand. This was someone their age, who they sort of knew, explaining what prejudice felt like from the other side. That horrible sense that if people were your enemy it meant they didn't feel, didn't breathe, didn't think like you did. Really, they were hardly proper *people* at all. So it was all right to drop bombs and destroy people's lives, or treat them no better than animals.

Except it wasn't.

The mood grew ever more sombre. By the time Esther finished talking, a few pupils were wiping their eyes. The rest of the class looked stunned.

'Thank you for listening,' Esther said, her chin held high. I was close enough to see the tiniest tremble in her bottom lip. And it made me think her even more magnificent.

It was Mrs Simmons who moved first, opening a

cupboard at the side of the room and bringing out half a dozen sewing tins.

'Right, class,' she said, all shrill again. 'Take a coat each from the piles. Unpick the stars *carefully* – no snagging of fabric, please – these are people's best coats, remember.'

Within moments, the room was noisy again, only this time with the buzz of activity. Each pupil had a coat spread in front of them on their desk. Some people got straight on with the task. Others took a moment to look at the garment, as if it was a person they were meeting for the first time. One boy, I noticed, lifted a sleeve to his nose and sniffed it. Another fastened the buttons and tidied the lapels.

Of the two coats left, I took one over to a spare desk and sat down. This coat was knee-length with a belt at the waist. It smelled of face powder and the sea. Made of grey wool with tiny red flecks in it, its buttons were shaped like budding roses, and I'd a feeling I'd seen Frau Berliner wearing it. With a few snips the star came off. After I'd smoothed away any trace of stitch marks on the fabric, it was, once again, just a coat. A lovely, elegant coat. All it told the world about Frau Berliner was that she had excellent taste.

It didn't take long to remove all the stars.

'What do we do with them now?' a boy at the front asked.

Mrs Simmons gestured to the coal stove that burned in a corner of the classroom. But Esther shook her head: 'Can everyone put their star into the pocket of the coat they removed it from, please?'

Mrs Simmons looked confused. 'Can't we throw them away?'

'They're not yours to get rid of,' Esther replied firmly. 'What happens to each of those stars now is entirely up to the person who had to wear it.'

She was right: those stars were other people's stories, not ours.

Then we had the task of delivering a huge heap of coats back to their owners. Returning them was much easier, mind you, because the whole class came with us to help.

*

It didn't change everything, not straight away. Twenty pupils unpicking yellow stars was just the beginning. Yet on my way home from school that afternoon Mrs Moore came out of her bakery to speak to me.

'I've been hearing *all* about you,' she said rather mysteriously. 'You and your friend were very brave, taking on the class like that. Bravo to you both.'

At school the next day, I told Esther. It was breaktime and we were sharing the jam sandwiches Ephraim insisted on putting in my satchel.

'Has anyone started speaking to you in the street?' I asked.

'The *street*?' She laughed, almost choking on her sandwich so I had to thump her on the back. 'They've been *queuing up* to meet Papa. Everyone's heard how he saved Cliff's life and now people are coming from the next village. Someone this morning even brought him their *cat*!'

I looked at her in amazement, especially when she told me the cat's owner was Mrs Wilcox the farmer.

'We need another idea now,' I said eagerly. 'Removing the stars made people think, but—'

'– we have to build on it. Bring people together,' Esther finished for me.

'Well, we bonded over jam sandwiches,' I said, holding up the empty paper wrapper.

Esther grinned. And just like that she had another brilliant plan, though I like to think Ephraim's sandwiches helped.

*

Esther's idea was to hold a tea party. So, working together at Queenie's kitchen table, we designed invitations on whatever scraps of card we could find. These we then delivered to all the villagers and the refugees, also asking them to bring cake or sandwiches to share. The party was to take place that Sunday afternoon. By chance it fell on the same day Cliff was due to leave hospital, which was brilliant because I knew he'd not want to miss it for the world.

All morning we set up tables in the village hall, with some of the Budmouth kids coming to help – boys called John, Clive and Arthur, and two girls, Gillian and Pamela. They'd brought snowdrops and early primroses, which we put in jugs, and white cloths that made the tables look smart. Meanwhile, Mrs Henderson and Miss Carter hung up a huge banner on the wall, which said, 'Welcome to Budmouth Point'.

I kept listening out for the Plymouth bus until Mrs Henderson said it didn't come until three thirty. Though I couldn't wait to see Mum and Cliff, I also knew that being together would make us notice who was missing. There was *still* no news on Sukie – not even a sighting. Maybe I was being over-sensitive, but

Miss Carter's cheerful reassurances were starting to sound rather strained.

At three o'clock the guests began arriving. I shook hands with Jim the cabbage man and Mr Barrowman as they came in. I said 'hullo' to people whose names I still didn't know; had a quick cuddle with baby Reuben, whose mum had brought him along; thanked everyone who'd come with plates of food, which I took and put on the white-clothed tables. In fact, I smiled so much it made my face ache.

As more of the refugees arrived, the Budmouth kids started whispering with interest. Pamela said to Gillian, 'That's the coat I unpicked,' and nodded at Mr Schoenman.

'That's mine,' Gillian replied. She was pointing at Fräulein Weber. Giggling shyly, she went over to say hullo.

Esther was busy showing people where to hang their things.

'You all right?' I asked as we passed each other.

She puffed out her cheeks. 'It's hard work being nice, isn't it?' Yet you could see she was loving every minute.

Even in our wildest dreams we hadn't expected so many to come. There had to be over a hundred people from Budmouth Point alone, and though the Austrians hovered a little tentatively around the edges still, Dr Wirth couldn't move for adoration.

I wouldn't have put it past Ephraim not to come at all. So I was awfully glad when he arrived. He'd made quite an effort too, wearing a smart grey suit and carrying a tin of homemade carrot fudge. He'd even tied a red ribbon round Pixie's neck. It crossed my mind he was hoping, on this big occasion, that Sukie might miraculously appear, like people did in stories and at the end of films. Or maybe that was wishful thinking on my part.

I was about to tell him how nice he looked when Pixie's barked. In a scrabble of paws, she shot off across the room to greet someone she knew who was coming in the door. The person was wearing short trousers that didn't cover his scabby knees, and my heart leaped because it was Cliff.

I rushed over at once to give him a hug, though it was hard to with Pixie squirming at his feet.

'Careful!' Cliff winced. 'Mind my stitches!'

'Hullo, darling.' Mum kissed me. 'He's tired, so we won't stay long.'

'I am here, you know,' Cliff remarked, grinning cheekily. He looked a million times better than when

I'd last seen him but was still very thin in the face. Once we'd got him comfortable in a chair, with Pixie at his feet, Mum went in search of tea.

'Want to see my scar?' Cliff asked, the minute she was gone.

I nodded eagerly.

Without a flicker of embarrassment, he untucked his shirt to show me the four-inch purple scar between his right hip and belly button, criss-crossed with thread where the stitches were still in.

'Cor!' I gasped. 'That's the wasp's ankles!'

'Isn't it?' Cliff looked extremely chuffed. Unfortunately, the hospital hadn't let him bring home his appendix in a pot, so he said, but it was all right because he could make his scar pull faces. 'Watch this, look!'

We were still laughing when Mum returned with two cups of tea. 'Olive, love, Mrs Henderson's asking if you'll pop down the road and fetch Queenie. She seems to have forgotten what the time is.'

'Her clocks are stopped, that's why,' Cliff explained. 'And all at the same time.'

'Still?' I asked. 'Last I heard Dr Wirth was trying to fix them. Maybe she doesn't want them working again.'

Mum looked surprised. 'Why ever not?' Then, as if

the answer had come to her, her face paled. 'Oh. Oh dear. The poor thing.'

'It's all right,' Cliff replied. 'They're not very nice clocks.'

Somehow, I didn't think that was what Mum meant.

EACH LITTLE ERROR GIVES YOUR ENEMY MORE TIME

Not wanting to miss a minute of the party, I ran all the way to Queenie's. The shop was shut up, so I let myself in through the back door.

'Queenie?' I called. 'We're about to serve the tea. Are you coming?'

After the crowded village hall, the house was quiet. The clock on the kitchen wall was still stopped; I wondered if Dr Wirth had given up trying to mend it.

'Queenie?'

Thinking she'd not heard me, I went down the cellar steps and found her sat at the table. With her sweater sleeves pushed up, she was going through what looked to be an old shoebox. She was crying.

I'd never seen Queenie in tears before: she wasn't the sort of person you'd imagine cried very much and it threw me, rather.

'I'm sorry.' I backed away. 'I'll wait upstairs,' but she was up and past me before I'd a chance to.

'Give me a moment,' she said.

I didn't know whether to wait. To be honest, she didn't look in the mood for a party and might prefer to be left alone. The contents of the shoebox lay spilled across the table like a mouse's nest. For that's all it seemed to be – a clump of shredded paper.

The paper was tissue-thin – airmail paper. The strips looked as though they'd once been letters, little phrases like *'with all my heart'* and *'I dream of you every day'* on each one. They reminded me of the lucky sayings you got in Christmas crackers or lines from the Valentine's cards Dad used to send Mum. Gently, I stirred the nest of paper with my hand. In doing so, I saw a few more:

each day without you is agony

my dearest Queenie do write soon

I'm sorry for the tears

don't forget how I love you

245

So Queenie *did* have a penpal after all – a sweetheart, by the looks of things. I felt a bit uncomfortable reading what was private so, scooping up the strips, I put them back in the box and closed the lid.

It was then I saw on the side of the box – a name, a date: 'Marcus Epstein: Frankfurt, March 2nd 1940'. It was today's date, a year ago. And, at the bottom, a specific time.

2.10 p.m.

'Romantic', Mrs Henderson had called Queenie's clocks; but to me, realising what it probably meant, it made my throat thicken with tears. No wonder Mum had understood what a stopped clock might mean.

Something must've happened to Marcus Epstein that day, at that time. Something terrible that made Queenie's life stop dead.

My brain tried to fill in the gaps. Perhaps Marcus was a Jew. Perhaps this was why she was so set on helping Jewish people, and had such guts when it came to standing up for what was decent.

I didn't know. In many ways it didn't matter. It was Queenie's private business. She was the person who'd thrown stones at German aircraft, and yet protected the injured pilot from more harm. She fought for people, that was what Queenie did. Beneath our race, our religion, we were all human beings. We all hurt in the same ways.

Upstairs in front of the hall mirror, I could hear her now repinning her hair and fastening her coat.

'Right, Olive, I'm ready,' she called down.

I went to join her, taking in her smooth, tearless face, the newly tidied hair. You'd never know from looking at her that her heart was still breaking. But that was the awful thing: life did go on, and so did that horrible empty ache you felt when someone wasn't there any more.

*

Back at the tea party, the hall buzzed with noise: laughter, different accents, the excited exclamations of people trying delicious new foods. It was nice to be amongst it again because it helped chase my sad thoughts away. I hoped Queenie, who was given a cup of tea by Mrs Henderson, was feeling the same.

Cliff and me, meanwhile, decided to have a competition to see who could get the most food on their plate in one go. Everyone had brought something, and seeing it all spread out on the table you'd have thought rationing had ended.

'I want to try everything,' I said to Cliff, whose eyes were on stalks.

There were jam sandwiches – naturally – cold chicken, slices of potato pie. And on the sweets table were cinnamon biscuits, Ephraim's carrot fudge, fruit scones, rock buns. What caught my eye most were the foods I didn't know, made by our Austrian visitors: the flat bread, the shredded cabbage in vinegar, the dark, dense cake dusted with icing sugar, and the apple pie that was oblong rather than round, and whose pastry crackled when you cut it.

'I'm *going* to try everything,' Cliff replied. I just hoped he wouldn't burst his stitches.

Half an hour later, feeling thoroughly sick, we stopped eating, and Cliff was declared the winner. Outside, the dusk was gathering but no one was in a rush to leave, the noise in the hall now the peaceful lull of easy chat. We moved our chairs so Dr Wirth and Esther could join us, and it felt nice just to talk about silly things like Pixie's doggy beard and whether the hospital had thrown Cliff's appendix away or if not, where it might be now. Mum hadn't mentioned going home early again, and no one reminded her.

Then Mrs Henderson clapped. 'Let's have dancing!'

Everyone got to their feet, dragging tables and chairs

aside to make space. Mr Geffen said he had sheet music in his suitcase, and went off to fetch it. When he came back, it turned out Mrs Moore knew most of the tunes on the piano.

At first it was only the Budmouth kids dancing, which was like watching carthorses charging about, until Esther grabbed the boy called John. Following her lead, Miss Carter took Clive, and together they showed them how to do a dance so fast it made my head spin. It was all kicking legs and swinging arms, with steps as goofy as a clown's. Even its name – the lindyhop – sounded jolly good fun.

I went over to Mum, taking her hands and pulling her up. 'Come on, let's give it a try.'

'Oh I can't, Olive,' she protested. 'It's too fast for me.' But she was laughing and not putting up much of a fight.

I managed to get her on to the dance floor. And we'd got as far as learning how to swing our arms, when the music suddenly stopped mid-beat. Everyone groaned.

A familiar voice boomed over the noise: 'Ephraim Pengilly? Are you present?'

Like a switch had dropped, the room went quiet. Mr Spratt in his navy coastguard's uniform stood just inside the door. With him were four policemen.

What were they here for? Who'd done something wrong? You could see the questions and suspicions returning to people's faces. Heart floundering, I guessed the answer: the authorities had got wind of thirty-two Austrians arriving in Budmouth Point by boat. In truth, it was bound to happen eventually; it was only a matter of time.

Mr Spratt pointed to Ephraim. 'That's our man.'

As he and the policemen strode across the room, we moved to its edges.

A glance passed between Mum and Miss Carter. Queenie stared straight ahead, unblinking. Mrs Henderson started fanning herself with her hand.

'I'm here,' Ephraim said clearly. And I saw how somehow we'd all drifted away from him, so he stood alone. Even Pixie had stayed traitorously close to Cliff, who'd gone back for thirds of cake.

It wasn't right. Not when Ephraim had done so much for Cliff and me – actually, for pretty much everyone in this room. Letting go of Mum, I went over and linked my arm with his.

'No, Olive.' He tried to pull away.

'Come come, now's not the time for heroics.' Mr Spratt rolled his eyes. 'Unless you'd like to be handcuffed together and *both* taken to the police station?'

I didn't move.

'Wait a minute. What's Ephraim actually done?' Queenie asked.

'It's what he *hasn't* done that concerns me. A boat turns up mysteriously from France, and not one word of an explanation in the lighthouse log book?' Mr Spratt put his little hands together. 'That, madam, goes against *all* regulations.'

Queenie's face flushed an angry red, but it was Mum who answered. 'I've also broken regulations,' she said levelly. I felt a thud of panic as she walked right up to Mr Spratt and held out her wrists. 'So if you're threatening my daughter with handcuffs, you'd better arrest me too.'

'And me,' Queenie joined her.

'Likewise, Mr Spratt,' agreed Mrs Henderson.

'You should take me as well,' added Miss Carter.

The policemen looked at each other, eyebrows raised.

'I've also broken the law.' A new voice called out from the other side of the hall. It was the schoolteacher, Mrs Simmons, now nervously on her feet. 'Last night, I forgot to close my blackout curtains.'

There was a pause.

Then Jim the cabbage man stood up. 'You'd better take me too, officer. I gave my petrol coupons to Mr Fairweather.'

'I bought a pair of nylons on the black market,' said Mrs Moore the baker, which raised eyebrows amongst her friends.

People were now standing up thick and fast. I didn't know whether to cheer or beg them to stop as the policemen started arguing over what to do.

Mr Spratt looked extremely uncomfortable. 'Look, if you'd all just sit down—'

'I fed my dog my meat ration,' a woman I didn't know called out.

Then Pamela stood up. 'I copied Gillian's history homework last week.'

'And I took that piece of chocolate you were hiding in your desk,' admitted Gillian.

'My baby boy drank too much milk.' This was Miriam with Reuben squirming in her arms. 'He's just over two weeks old. Do you wish to handcuff him as well?'

It was so absurd that people started to see the funny side of what was happening. Even the policemen had taken their hats off and were scratching their heads. One of them was drinking a cup of tea someone had offered him. The funniest thing of all, though, was the expression on Mr Spratt's face. He'd gone such a violent shade of purple, I honestly thought he'd burst.

'These people shouldn't be punished for their kindness,' said Dr Wirth, who, stopping in front of Mr Spratt, stood a good foot taller. 'You should be proud of what they've done. I only wish more of my fellow countrymen had such humanity.'

'My dad's right. You've all made us welcome here,' Esther agreed. She caught my eye and smiled.

Trying hard to appear dignified, Mr Spratt looked Dr Wirth up and down. 'I'm afraid we haven't been introduced, Mr – ?'

'*Dr* Wirth. And *I'm afraid* you'll need to arrest us as well,' he said, gesturing to the other refugees.

Confusion spread over Mr Spratt's face. He looked to the policemen, then to Ephraim, Mum and the others stood before him.

'Don't be ridiculous, man!' he fumed. 'We can't possibly arrest you *all*!'

'Not on a Sunday,' remarked the policeman with the teacup in his hand.

His colleague agreed. 'We're not going to break up a happy party, either.'

The only thing left for Mr Spratt to do was leave, which he did, storming out, nostrils flaring like a small, squat bull.

There was a beat of quiet as the room settled again.

We caught each other's eyes. Smiled. Laughed. Then hands, hats, napkins flew into the air. The cheer of delight that went up with them was enough to lift the roof.

V FOR VICTORY

It had never been the refugees' plan to stay long in Budmouth Point. Although in the end they'd got a warm welcome here, our country's immigration laws were not so friendly. Without official visas the Jews were termed 'enemy aliens', which to me sounded like more nasty name-calling: technically it meant they weren't supposed to be here. Over the following days a few more of the refugees left – Mr Geffen headed to Canada, Miriam and Reuben, Elise and Jakob for America. Realistically I knew it wouldn't be long before Esther and Dr Wirth went on their way too.

Meanwhile, knowing Sukie was still on the other side of the Channel made missing her even harder. German-occupied France was a dangerous place. No one had heard from her. No one could get hold of her, though Miss Carter, still blaming herself, tried every possible avenue. I think she even considered sending a pigeon.

I felt hopeless because there was nothing I could do. It was unbearable to think we'd come this far and Sukie might not make it home safely. Yet much as I adored my sister, I was beginning to understand Mum's view too. Sukie was brilliant, but she wasn't necessarily careful. The fact she'd travelled all the way to France then *missed* the boat home was a rather good example of it. Yet as much as Sukie was careless, she was brave and resourceful, so we shouldn't have been surprised that she eventually found her way back to us in the manner she did.

*

One morning, as was often the case, I woke very early. It was soon after Cliff had come out of hospital. Not strong enough to face the lighthouse ladder yet, he was staying at Mrs Henderson's with Mum, and I'd not quite got used to having the bedroom to myself. I'd read all my books from home countless times, and the ones on the shelves above our beds. Knowing I'd not be able to get back to sleep, I decided to go for a walk.

'Coming, girl?' I whispered to Pixie, who was stretched out on Cliff's bed. She opened one disinterested eye, which I took to mean 'no'. Pulling on a cardigan over my nightgown, I grabbed my coat and shoes and tiptoed down the stairs.

Outside, it was just getting light. There was no one about, only gulls circling the harbour, which was always a sign the fishing boats were due back soon. For once, there wasn't even a breeze. The sea was flat, silky-looking, the same pinks and blues and oranges as the sky.

Dropping on to the beach, I started walking. I'd not been down here since the refugees arrived, and the crunch of shingle underfoot brought back to me, vividly, the drama and panic of that night. Only twelve refugees were left in Budmouth. It was mid-March now, which meant they'd been here almost a month. They'd settled well; in a way it felt like they'd always lived here. And on a day like today, when the sea was kind and the sky bright, it was easy to forget anything bad or dangerous had happened – *was* still happening across the Channel in Europe.

At this time of day, the tide was a long way out, making the beach seem wider and flatter than usual. Before long I'd reached the groyne, where I stopped to gaze out to sea.

I heard the engine first – a chugging, spluttering – that for a split second made my heart stop. But boat engines, I was learning, sounded different from aeroplanes. The boat rounding the headland was the first of the fishing fleet returning to harbour. You could tell the catch was good from the way the hull sat low in the water. It passed close enough to shore for me to see the men on board, laughing and joking with each other. One of them waved to me – a proper, gleeful, two-armed wave above his head. It made me smile as I waved back.

By the time I reached the harbour again the fishing boat was already moored up. The men had unloaded their nets and were stacking boxes of silvery fish on the quay. It was an impressive, delicious sight and got me thinking about mackerel on toast for breakfast. So I wasn't paying a huge amount of attention when someone called out, 'Olive? Is that you?'

I froze to the spot. I'd have known that voice anywhere.

'I can't believe it!' she cried.

It stunned me. I couldn't believe it, either. But there was no mistaking who it was.

I didn't even get a proper look at her. She threw herself at me with such force we both fell backwards across the cobbles. The person holding on to me was soaking wet, and terribly in need of a bath. I didn't care. I clung to her as tight as she clung to me.

'I saw you on the beach,' Sukie mumbled against my neck. 'I was on the fishing boat, waving ...' She was sobbing and laughing all at once. So was I.

When at last we pulled apart, I looked at her properly, and thought for one awful moment there'd been a mistake. This wasn't my sister at all, but a stranger. Last time I'd seen her she'd had curled hair, face powder, lipstick, the works. Now she was wearing trousers and a man's tweed jacket, with a woolly hat pulled down over her hair.

'I'm not looking my best, am I?' Sukie joked feebly.

It didn't matter; none of that silly stuff mattered.

'I'm just so glad to see you,' I whispered.

'Me too,' she said, cupping my face in her freezing-cold hands.

'What ... I mean ... how ... ?' I managed to say. There was so much I had to ask her I didn't know where to start.

The fishermen had stopped unloading their catch to watch us. It was funny how they gazed at Sukie as if she was their favourite, long-lost daughter.

One of them called out: 'Caught more than fish today, didn't we, eh?'

I recognised him. He was the man who'd argued with Queenie about the lighthouse. Who'd told Mr

Barrowman to shut up over the German pilot. I'd had him down as an old curmudgeon, but not any more: he was the man who'd brought my sister safely home.

I stared at Sukie. 'Where did they find you?'

Sukie laughed her lovely tinkly laugh. 'Oh, adrift in the Channel in a rowing boat. They rescued me late last night – it was a stroke of absolute luck. I can't thank these dear chaps enough.'

It was just how things were with Sukie: even in the middle of the English Channel she'd found people willing to help her. This time, though, she'd been the one trying to help others, and she'd risked her life doing it.

*

It was easier – and warmer – to go straight back to Mrs Henderson's. She made tea and crumpets and banked up the sitting-room fire so it quickly grew stifling. Sukie, in borrowed dry clothes, her hair wrapped in a towel, sat as close as she could to the hearth to get warm. We didn't mean to wake everyone, but it wasn't long before Cliff came downstairs. His face was an absolute picture when he saw Sukie. Throwing his arms around her, he stared at her, speechless.

'Can we go to the cinema again?' was the first thing he managed to say. 'A proper trip that lasts more than ten minutes?'

The next footsteps on the stairs were Mum's. Seeing the chair pulled up to the hearth, she stopped in the doorway.

'Hullo, Mum.' Sukie, rather sheepishly, stood up.

'Oh, Sukie,' Mum said quietly. 'You silly, silly girl.'

I braced myself for the hugs. The kisses. The happy tears. Cliff's favourite bits in films were when long-lost people got reunited, yet this was real life, concerning people we loved.

Mum, though, wasn't smiling.

'You weren't well. The doctor told you to rest, didn't he? No work, no stress – that's what he said,' Sukie tried to explain.

'Oh, my darling girl,' Mum murmured. 'I've been so desperately worried about you.'

Sukie started crying. 'I was only trying to help. I knew you wouldn't want to let anyone down.'

When they hugged it was like watching two people cling to each other for dear life. It was quite overwhelming – and so typical of Mum and Sukie, whose love for each other was always the boldest, fiercest kind.

Eventually, they sat down on the settee. Sukie, her feet tucked under her, leaned against Mum.

'I've got some explaining to do,' Sukie admitted, addressing me. 'I'm so sorry I left you and Cliff during the air raid. I shouldn't have shouted when you came after me.'

Knowing what I knew now, it made sense that she had. Me calling 'Sukie' at the top of my voice, when she was pretending to be Mrs Arby, would've blown her cover.

'I ended up with Mum's coat,' I told her. 'And I found the note you'd hidden in it. So we managed – eventually – to work out what you were up to.'

I could sense her looking at me – *really* looking, like she was seeing something new. 'You clever old stick,' she said finally, which made me stupidly pleased. Then she unwrapped the towel from her head and shook out her damp hair.

'Good grief!' Mum gasped. 'Your beautiful hair!'

'It's so ... *short*!' Cliff cried.

Actually, it wasn't much shorter than mine. But you could see lumps hacked out of it – a haircut done in a hurry.

'I had to,' Sukie explained. 'It was a disguise to get past the soldiers.'

Cliff looked aghast. 'I've never seen a boy with hair

like *that.*'

Personally, I thought it looked daringly glamorous, especially on Sukie. Mum ran her hand over it like she was stroking a cat.

'Why do you get yourself into these scrapes?' she said, though not unkindly. 'You didn't even have the good sense to catch the right boat home again.'

'I didn't miss the boat on purpose, Mum,' Sukie replied. 'I met someone and our meeting took longer than expected. You see, the man, Monsieur Bonet, knew Dad.'

Mum's hand fell into her lap. 'How?'

'He was with him at the end.'

I covered my mouth, but Sukie reached for my hand and clasped it tightly in hers. I hoped some of her courage would seep into me because I wasn't sure I was ready for what she had to say next.

UNITED WE ARE STRONGER

Sukie told us what had happened to Dad. Once or twice, I almost asked her to stop, but I had to know – we all had to know – how he died. Otherwise, we'd be stuck wondering for ever.

Dad had been flying back to England, not far from the French coast, when his plane got hit by enemy gunfire. It tore a huge hole in the tail of his plane, killing his gunner and two other crew members outright.

Rapidly losing height, the damaged aircraft was heading straight for the town of Tollevast. Monsieur Bonet, who Sukie said was an old man who kept chickens, saw it happen before his very eyes: how Dad managed to keep the plane up as it flew over the houses, before coming down with a thump in Monsieur Bonet's orchard.

The most heartbreaking part was that Dad walked away from the crash. He surrendered himself to Monsieur Bonet, who'd gone running down the orchard to help him, not arrest him.

But there were injuries inside Dad that weren't obvious straight away. He made it as far as the kitchen of the farmhouse. He even started to drink a cup of brandy, and was telling Monsieur Bonet in his schoolboy French about his family, back at home. For good luck, Dad always carried a photo of us in his shirt pocket when he flew, and he got it out to show Monsieur Bonet. It was taken a couple of years ago when we'd gone to Brighton on a day trip, and me and Cliff are eating ice creams and Mum's got her eyes shut. Sukie's the only one of us who looks normal. Putting down his cup, Dad said he had a headache. He died right there in the chair.

Not wanting the Nazis to take Dad's body, Monsieur Bonet buried him in a quiet spot in his orchard. He reported the crashed plane to the authorities and said that all on board were killed, even handing over Dad's identity tags to cover himself. The photo he kept, in the hope that one day he'd be able to trace the pilot's family.

When, a few months later, he heard rumours of an English woman helping Jews escape across the Channel, Monsieur Bonet tracked Sukie down to carry a message back to England. He recognised her as soon as he saw her. Hearing his story and seeing the photo, Sukie knew without doubt who the pilot was buried in this old man's orchard, in a sunny spot under an apple tree.

After Sukie had finished talking, I sat staring into space, not crying but aware of an ache deep inside my chest. I thought to myself: this pain is my heart breaking.

I don't know how long I sat there, but at some point the pain began to ease. I was able to feel something else – a sort of gladness, I suppose – that Dad died gently and quietly in a kind old man's kitchen. And in a way we were with him at the end; at least our photo was.

It was late morning by now. Word of Sukie's arrival had reached Queenie and Miss Carter, who were in the kitchen with Mrs Henderson, the sounds and smells of breakfast drifting down the hall.

Outside, the sun was shining. It was shaping up to be a beautiful March day. One wall of Mrs Henderson's sitting room was almost entirely made up of windows that looked out over fields where her goats grazed. It made a pleasant change from gazing out to sea.

'Look!' Cliff said, pointing to a clump of trees that grew close to the house. 'They've got buds on. That means spring's coming, doesn't it?'

'Ephraim says spring always comes early in Devon,' I replied. At the mention of his name, I could've sworn I saw Sukie blush.

'Monsieur Bonet says we're welcome to visit Dad's grave when it's safe to do so,' she said, taking Mum's hand. 'Honestly Mum, it's a gorgeous spot. I think you'll love it.'

Mum frowned at their entwined fingers like she was about to disagree. Maybe it was all this talk of buds and daffodils, but when she looked up, she was smiling. 'I'd like that, darling. I think we all would.'

*

We ate the sort of breakfast fit for soldiers after battle. There was porridge with cream and honey, eggs, toast, bacon for those who wanted it. On finally seeing Sukie in daylight, Miss Carter was at first too embarrassed to eat.

'I'm so sorry,' she kept saying, going pink. 'I don't know what I was thinking. It was unforgivable.'

'You need new spectacles,' Mrs Henderson said helpfully. 'Getting the message wrong was one thing, but look – the girl's half her mother's age – no offence meant.'

Sukie and Mum both laughed. Even with their different hair, they did look confusingly similar. It was Sukie whose smile dazzled, though. And I could see Miss Carter gazing at her, thinking her completely marvellous. I just hoped Ephraim, when he finally met Sukie in person, would think the same.

Queenie, meanwhile, was already arranging to bring in another refugee boat from France. She wouldn't be put off by the threat Mr Spratt posed.

'That silly little man's the least of our worries.' She shovelled food into her mouth as she talked. 'My sense is that Hitler's plans for the Jews are only just beginning. These next few months we're going to be busy.'

'Whatever you decide, count me in,' Sukie said.

There was a chorus of agreement around the table. And it really did help, feeling part of those plans. It reminded me there was a future, and we'd all be involved in it. We weren't going to be beaten by hate.

*

Though it wasn't quite that straightforward. When things had quietened down, Mr Spratt sent the police back to Budmouth Point. Of everyone, only Queenie was charged – for forgery of documents – then given a suspended sentence, which meant she didn't have to go to prison. This was especially good news because now Esther had got all her clocks working, they had to be wound every Sunday on the dot. Only Queenie herself could be trusted with this important job.

Mum, looking stronger by the day, went back to London. She said she'd be all right with Gloria for company, and anyway thought it time she returned to work. We didn't ask if she'd gone back to the office in Shoreditch – that sort of thing was secret – there was a war on, after all.

Ephraim was a harder nut to crack. Seeing Sukie in the flesh, he was convinced she was too good for him and retreated, hermit-like, further into his shell.

'Crikey,' Cliff said, fancying himself an expert on romance suddenly. 'Why don't they just kiss and get it over with?'

'It's not like in the movies,' I told him.

Though actually, in the end, it sort of was. Knowing Ephraim's weakness for dogs and messages in writing, Sukie trained Pixie to carry a note to Ephraim, inviting him to the cinema on a date. And so they went to see a new film called *Gone with the Wind* or something equally slushy, and came home so lovey-dovey I hardly knew where to look.

After Queenie's arrest, the remaining refugees decided, amongst themselves, to do things properly. As Dr Wirth reminded us, they'd never planned to stay in Budmouth Point for ever. They handed themselves in to the authorities and were taken to an 'internment camp' at Croyde on the north Devon coast. Someone said it'd once been a holiday camp, and weren't they lucky, though I don't think they saw it that way. Esther didn't go with her father – as a Kindertransport child her papers were valid – and she stayed on at Queenie's so she could continue with school.

One day in the Easter holidays, Esther and I caught the bus to visit Croyde. We carried with us bottles of goats' milk from Mrs Henderson, who'd insisted we take something nice for our Jewish friends. It was a warm day, and the journey took for ever, the roads twisting up over Dartmoor and plunging down the other side again. All the while, the goats' milk got lumpier and smellier.

'It'll be cheese by the time we get there,' Esther moaned.

The camp certainly didn't look like a place you'd

visit on holiday. Our friends weren't the only refugees there, either. In total there were eighty or more who'd fled Hitler. Though it was on a clifftop overlooking the sea, it was dusty and rundown and surrounded by a barbed-wire fence.

'But only a *low* barbed-wire fence,' Dr Wirth pointed out. 'We're no security risk to the English; we hate Hitler as much as you do.'

In fact, he told us, some of the refugees were joining what was called the Pioneer Corps, where they'd be doing special war duties for the British against the enemy.

Seeing how overjoyed Esther was to be with her father brought tears to my eyes. It was wonderful to see the others too, who hugged us and said hadn't we grown and made us eat apple cake and thanked us for the lumpy milk.

Inside the camp were rows of wooden huts where everyone lived. They'd hung scarves at the windows and spread bright blankets on their beds in an attempt to make things more homely. Mr Schoenman had set up a bread oven to bake special loaves every Friday for Sabbath. Fräulein Weber was teaching Hebrew, the newspaper writers running a newsletter of sorts. Mimi Schoenman and her sisters Anna and Rosa had made the most amazing tree house in a hollowed-out ash tree.

'It could be worse,' Frau Berliner said, forcing a smile.

It wasn't their home, though. It felt unfair to see these people we'd tried so hard to help still living in a way they didn't deserve.

*

Later, on the bus back to Budmouth Point, Esther said the news from Austria wasn't good.

'Father believes they got away just in time. There are Nazi camps now that people don't come back from. They're being rounded up and sent away by train – not just a few people, Olive, but *thousands* at a time. He doesn't think we'll return to Vienna. When the war's over we're going to live in America.' She didn't seem in the least excited at the prospect: she sounded exhausted.

We were quiet for the rest of the journey. As the bus turned off the main road for the coast, I sat up a little taller in my seat.

'Look at the lighthouse.' I nudged Esther. 'Isn't it beautiful?'

Today, in full sunlight, you could see its red and white stripes beginning to show through the peeling grey paint. Mr Spratt had wanted it repainted, but this time no one volunteered.

'A beacon to guide the lost to safety,' Miss Carter once said about the lighthouse.

Sitting here with Esther Wirth I felt as if I'd found safety. One of us, at least, had her dad back. I, meanwhile, had Sukie, Mum, Cliff; the rest of Budmouth Point I was just beginning to get to know. As our bus made its lazy way down the hill I felt a pang of love for this funny little village by the sea that I now called home.

*

That night after supper, I was too tired to even open my book.

'Go to bed,' Sukie ordered. 'I'll do the washing-up.'

Thinking what she really wanted was some time alone with Ephraim, I dutifully went downstairs to our room, where Cliff was already fast asleep, Pixie at his feet.

Getting into bed I wasn't expecting to fall asleep. As I lay there, I spotted my seashell on the windowsill, and thought how I didn't really listen to it these days, not when I could hear the real sea sighing and swooshing over the rocks below. It never sounded like that inside the shell.

To my great surprise, my eyelids soon felt heavy. Quite quickly, I grew sleepier, my mind flitting between Esther, the yellow stars, Ephraim's log book, Mum – all that had happened since we'd come to Budmouth Point. I still didn't understand everything. People, it seemed to me, were much harder to crack than codes. Yet it didn't matter where we came from, our language, our nationality, or our religion. As long as we all looked to the light.

'Goodnight, Dad,' I mumbled into my pillow.

The sounds of the sea grew distant. I think I fell asleep then, picturing Dad at the bottom of my bed, elbows leaning on the frame. Or maybe I was still awake. All I know is what I heard, the sound of his voice, so clear he might've really been here: 'Nighty night, old girl, sleep tight.'

Which, for the first time in ages, I did.

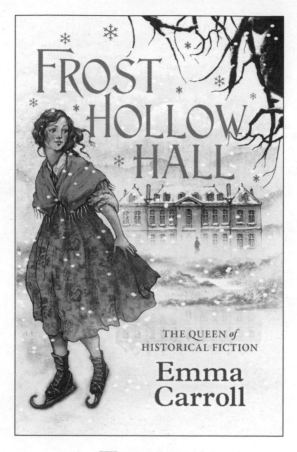

FROST HOLLOW HALL

THE QUEEN *of* HISTORICAL FICTION

Emma Carroll

WINTER, 1881

When Tilly Higgins falls through the ice whilst
skating she is rescued by the ghost of Kit Barrington,
who drowned at Frost Hollow Hall ten years ago.

And he desperately needs her help . . .

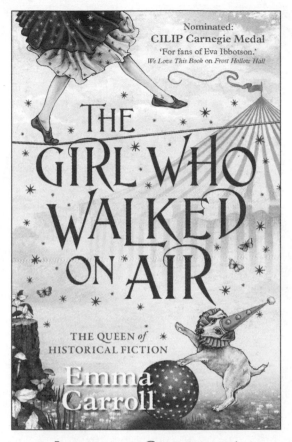

LADIES AND GENTLEMEN!
We bring you the sensational story of Louie
Reynolds, whose dream is to be a circus showstopper.
Yet the path to fame is a rocky one. Louie must find
the courage to become . . .
The Girl Who Walked on Air.

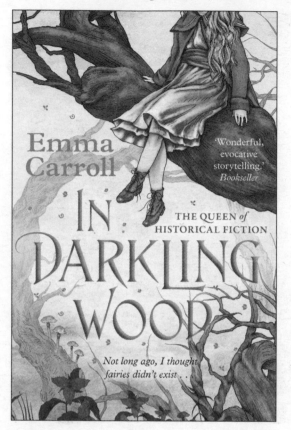

A phone call brings news that could save Alice's
brother's life . . . Back in 1918, the War over, another
girl awaits her brother's return from the front.
Neither girl must give up hope. At the bottom of
their garden is Darkling Wood, a place full of magic,
secrets and salvation. If you believe in fairies that is.

It's Christmas Eve, and Pearl Granger is making a
snow sister. It won't bring her real sister back. But a
snow sister is better than no sister.

Then a mysterious letter arrives, with a surprise that
will stir the heart of Pearl's family.

Will Christmas ever be the same again?

Tonight, at the Villa Diodati, there will be ghost stories that promise to 'freeze the blood'. As darkness falls, the storytelling begins. Then a girl is discovered on the doorstep. She's travelled a long way to tell her tale, and now they must listen.

But be warned: hers is no ordinary ghost story. Sometimes the truth is far more terrifying.